Split Decision

By Belle Payton

Simon Spotlight

New York London Toronto Sydney New Delhi

SIMON SPOTLIGHT
An imprint of Simon & Schuster Children's Publishing Division
1230 Avenue of the Americas, New York, New York 10020
This Simon Spotlight edition June 2016
Text by Heather Alexander
© 2016 by Simon & Schuster, Inc.
All rights reserved, including the right of reproduction in whole or in part in any form.
SIMON SPOTLIGHT and colophon are registered trademarks of
Simon & Schuster, Inc.
For information about special discounts for bulk purchases, please
contact Simon & Schuster Special Sales at 1-866-506-1949 or
business@simonandschuster.com.
Designed by Ciara Gay
The text of this book was set in Garamond.
Manufactured in the United States of America 0516 FFG
10 9 8 7 6 5 4 3 2 1
ISBN 978-1-4814-5267-0 (hc)
ISBN 978-1-4814-5266-3 (pbk)
ISBN 978-1-4814-5268-7 (eBook)
Library of Congress Catalog Card Number 2015938114

CHAPTER ONE

Alex Sackett checked her reflection in the screen of her phone.

"Seriously, Alex?" Emily Campbell scrunched her nose. "It's pizza. And studying for science. You look fine."

"But that's it. It's not *just* pizza and studying." Alex twirled a strand of her long hair around her finger, then released the chocolate-brown tendril and watched it bounce into place. Should she apply more lip gloss? Or were her lips too shellacked? Maybe she should wipe some off?

"We don't know for sure he'll be here," Emily said, pulling open the door of Sal's Pizzeria.

"But you said Greg said they were stopping

by—" Alex sucked in her breath. "Oh! Lindsey's here."

Their friend Lindsey Davis sat in a booth next to eighth-grade baseball player Johnny Morton. Her long blond hair fell over one eye. She reached for a mozzarella stick from the plate between them, laughing at something Johnny said. He laughed too.

Alex felt her stomach twist. "Are they—are they on a date?" she whispered.

"Of course! They're going out, you know that. Hey, Lindz!" Emily waved. Alex raised her hand too.

Lindsey waved but didn't call them over. *It must really be a date,* Alex decided.

Alex and Emily slid into an empty booth on the other side of the pizzeria. Alex couldn't take her eyes off Lindsey and Johnny. He said something. Then she said something. Back and forth. No awkward pauses. And they were both crazy good-looking. It was so unfair! Lindsey made having a boyfriend look so easy!

Alex had met Lindsey and Emily as soon as she'd moved to Ashland, Texas, this past summer. Lindsey was going out with Corey O'Sullivan then. And now she was going out with Johnny.

Last week Emily and Greg Fowler became an official couple. Their other friend, Rosa Navarro, was going out with Ryan O'Hara. Greg and Ryan didn't seem all that special, but still . . . . was Alex the only seventh-grade girl at Ashland Middle School without a boyfriend? It sure seemed that way. Well, her and her twin sister, Ava.

Great, Alex thought. She didn't need *this* to be a Sackett Twin thing too.

But Ava didn't want a boyfriend. She only wanted to play sports with the guys.

"Oh, wow!" Alex clapped her hand over her mouth. She hadn't meant to say that out loud. But Lindsey and Johnny had just *kissed*! Right in the middle of the pizza place!

"See?" Emily giggled. "I told you Lindsey was over Corey. He's all yours."

Alex sighed. Corey O'Sullivan, with his mischievous bright-blue eyes and dark-red hair, was far from all hers. Alex had liked him forever, but he'd been going out with Lindsey. Until now. Until Johnny . . . and that kiss.

Suddenly Alex felt queasy. "Have you and Greg kissed?" she whispered to Emily.

Emily blushed and looked away. "What do you think?"

Alex hadn't thought about it until now. But yes, she *did* think they had kissed. In fact, she was sure that all her friends not only had a boyfriend but had been kissed as well. Everyone except her.

She had been so close, too—and with Corey. They had been at his Christmas party, standing right under the mistletoe. He'd leaned toward her, and she'd closed her eyes, and . . . then it had started to snow. Everyone around them screamed with excitement and ran outside and *poof*! The moment was gone.

Now she wondered if he'd he really been leaning in to kiss her, or if she'd made it up. Maybe he was just going to tell her something. Doubt gnawed at her.

Alex exhaled loudly. When she had a problem, she hated to sit around and mope. Instead she flew into action. And that's what she would do now. She made a mental plan:

Get a boyfriend.

Get kissed.

How hard could that be?

It shouldn't be that hard, Alex decided. *After all, there are hundreds of boys at Ashland*

Middle School. But she didn't want just any boyfriend. She wanted Corey. Corey was popular, played football, and had the best smile in their grade. Alex shook her head. Her parents said she always aimed high. Of course, they meant with grades and activities. *I guess I aim high with boyfriends, too.*

Emily had promised to help her. They were at Sal's Pizzeria on a Monday night, pretending to study, because Emily heard Corey would be here. Alex knew Corey liked her. He'd been hanging around her locker, and laughing when she made jokes that she knew weren't funny. But maybe she'd completely misread things. Or maybe things had changed. It had been a while since his Christmas party, and she'd been so busy organizing and eventually performing in the school Variety Show that she hadn't spent much time with him.

The bell above the door jangled, and Corey, Greg, and Tim Fowler hurried in, shaking off the late February rain from their jackets. At the sight of him, Alex wished she'd had time to make a more detailed plan. How exactly was she supposed to get Corey to be her boyfriend? She'd never been a on a date before. Were there some magic words girls like Lindsey knew? A secret look? An emoji to text?

"Showtime!" Emily whispered to Alex. Then she waved the boys over.

Alex smiled brightly at Corey. Was she grinning like a demonic clown? She rearranged her face into a cool, *hey there* look and tried to lean casually against the back of the booth. Emily expertly maneuvered the boys so Corey had no choice but to slide next to Alex, while Greg and Tim squeezed in next to Emily.

Corey barely glanced at Lindsey and Johnny, Alex noticed. That had to be a good sign, right? Her heart beat so loudly she was sure the others could hear it.

Corey touched the cover of her textbook. "Do you have that science quiz tomorrow too? I can never remember that whole class, order, phylum thing."

For a moment, Alex thought about pretending that she didn't know it either. But she *did* know it. She wasn't going to play dumb. "I can help," she offered. "It's kingdom, phylum, class, order, family, genus, species."

"Oh yeah, you're a big help!" Corey raised

his arms in surrender. "How am I supposed to remember all that?"

"Use a mnemonic," Alex said. "I love making up mnemonics."

"Okay, you've totally lost me," Corey joked.

"Alex is always using big words to impress us," Emily said.

"I'm not trying to impress anyone," Alex insisted. She collected words the way some kids collected snow globes or postcards from faraway places. She loved the way so many different words could all mean the same thing. She loved certain letter combinations. How cool were the *m* and *n* together in mnemonic, especially since the *m* was silent?

Would Corey think this was cool too? Alex wasn't so sure. She knew he was smart, but she didn't know if he was as nerdy deep down as she was. She suddenly felt nervous. And when she was nervous, she talked. A lot.

"A mnemonic is when you take the first letters of each word and make a sentence to help you remember something," Alex explained to Corey. "Here's one: Kevin's Poor Cow Only Feels Good Sometimes. Or you can use King Phillip Cried Out For Good Soup."

Corey nodded vigorously. "Give me a sec." He thought a moment. "Keep Purple Cats Off Football Game Socks!"

"Wow, that one's hilarious! Totally ingenious!" Alex cringed. Why hadn't she just said "funny" and "smart"? She was messing up royally.

But soon Emily, Tim, and Greg were making up silly mnemonics too. Corey gave her a playful shove as he recited another one, and her heart sped up again. He was so close she could smell the fabric softener on his faded blue shirt—it was the same one her parents used. If they went out, he would sit even closer. He would hold her hand. And maybe kiss her.

"Alex? Hey, Earth to Alex!" Emily waved her hand in front of Alex's face.

Oh no! She'd been sitting there with her mouth hanging open. She hated how weird and awkward she got around boys, and she thought things had been getting better now that she was getting to know Corey a little more. But here she was, unable to speak and having a silent heart attack.

"What?" Alex asked. She fidgeted, readjusting her stretchy hot-pink headband.

"I was talking about that new movie, *Escape*

from Dark Woods. Aren't you dying to see it too?" Emily asked.

Alex wasn't dying to see it. She hated horror movies. Emily knew that.

"Well—" Alex started.

"Corey wants to see it," Emily interrupted. She shot Alex a meaningful look.

Alex brightened. "Yes! I do want to see it."

"You two should see it *together.*" Emily grinned.

"Hey, are you kids ordering a pizza?" Sal, the bearded owner, appeared at their table and wiped his hands on his white apron.

"Definitely. We'll have a large pie," Emily said. "Right, guys?"

Tim and Greg fell into a debate with Emily about pizza toppings, and Corey nudged her arm.

"Do you . . . um . . . want to go see that movie?" Corey asked in a low voice.

Alex wondered if she should play it cool, but she didn't think she could. "With you?"

"Yeah." Corey fiddled with a paper napkin.

Alex thought her face would crack if she dared to smile any bigger. Corey had asked her out!

"Definitely," she said.

"So you're good with mushrooms, Alex?" Tim asked. "Emily said you're a vegetarian."

Who cared what was on the pizza? She was finally going on a date! Her first date!

Ava Sackett let the sounds and smells of the Ashland Middle School gym envelop her as she rolled the basketball between her palms. She'd missed the familiar scent of sweat and excitement and the rhythmic pounding of sneakers. She'd missed the exhilaration of moving the ball up court and the heart-pounding thrill of scoring. She felt as if she'd returned home after a long journey. The world made so much more sense to her when she stood on a football field or basketball court.

"Hey, Sackett!" Xander Browning pumped his fist, as the boys' basketball team completed their final cooldown lap.

"I'm back!" Ava waved and smiled. Last week, when the doctor finally cleared her to play, she had literally jumped for joy. Nursing her sprained ankle at home while the season progressed without her had been torturous. In a few minutes, she would take the court with the Ashland Middle School girls' basketball team for her first practice in weeks. She still had to wear an ankle brace while she played, but she'd gotten pretty used to doing everything normally in it.

Ava watched Xander down his blue sports drink in two huge gulps and Kal Tippett wrap his green towel around his head. The boys' post-practice rituals were so familiar to her that she momentarily felt as if she belonged out there with them. She had played football with so many of these boys in the fall. She knew them far better than she knew the girls on the basketball team. She'd missed much of the season with her injury, and she'd just moved to Ashland over the summer, so she hadn't gotten very friendly with many of her teammates.

Ava dribbled the ball with one hand and gave Kal and Xander high fives with the other as they filed off the court.

"Ready to tear it up out there?" Xander asked.

"I was born ready!" Ava called. A group of eighth-grade girls in royal-blue-and-orange Ashland Tiger Cub sweatshirts and basketball shorts entered the gym.

"Watch out for her, Tamara," Kal said to the tallest of the girls. "We've made Ava football-tough."

"You didn't make me anything," Ava retorted with a grin. "I came on the field tougher than all of you."

"Burn!" called Xander. "She got you, Kal."

"Got you, too, Browning," Kal replied, and shoved Xander. Xander shoved him back as the boys jostled their way out of the gym and into the darkening Texas night.

Ava felt the girls eye her warily. She self-consciously tucked a stray piece of her chocolate-brown hair behind her ear. She didn't want them to get the wrong idea, especially on her first day back. She knew she was a good player, but she wasn't conceited. The football team had a bragging banter that she just fell into naturally.

"Your ankle's better now?" asked Tamara Baker.

"Totally. I'm dying to play with all of you," Ava said. "I can't believe I got hurt as soon as I hit the court in the first game. I was so bummed."

While Ava sat out, she had watched as Tamara became the team high scorer—she had even scored more points than their captain, Callie Wagner. She stood almost a full head taller than the other girls. Freckles covered her nose and cheeks, and her long blond braid reached down her back.

Tamara licked her lips and studied Ava. "We haven't done so badly without your 'Sackett magic,' you know. We've won eight games."

"I do know! That's great!" Ava gave her a genuine smile. She wasn't exactly sure what Tamara meant by "Sackett magic." She supposed Tamara was referring to the fact that Ava's dad was the new coach of the high school football team—that was why their family had moved from Massachusetts—and the team had won state this year. Coaching a high school football team to state victory in Texas was like successfully landing the first rocket on Mars—maybe even better. The whole town loved him now.

Except the Kelly/Baker family.

Ava hadn't realized right away that Tamara was a part of that family. And when she had, Tamara's competitiveness made a lot more sense.

Her older cousin, PJ Kelly, was the star high school quarterback. Her younger brother, Andy Baker, was on the middle school football team with Ava. He seemed to have the most issues with a girl on the team, even after Ava had proved herself to all the other guys. Various other Kelly and Baker cousins were head cheerleaders, marching band captains, and pep squad leaders. And then there was PJ's dad—Mr. Kelly hated Coach Sackett. Ava couldn't figure out why. The team had won and his son was QB1. What more did the man want? But Mr. Kelly's anti-Sackett feelings had infected the entire family. Including Tamara, it now seemed.

"On the court!" boomed Coach Rader. He clapped his hands, and the entire team began to jog and dribble balls around the perimeter of the gym. Ava fell into line.

The majority of the girls were in eighth grade, but there were a few other seventh graders in addition to Ava. She eagerly followed the warm-up drills, most of which she remembered from her two weeks of practice before hurting her ankle. She knew she'd be sore tomorrow, and she was glad. She felt like her old self again—full of energy.

The girls broke into a two-line layup drill. Tamara, in the spot ahead of her, netted the ball. For a moment, Ava worried if her time away from the court would show. But her first shot swooshed easily into the basket. Her second and third found the net too.

Tamara scored. Ava scored. Soon it felt as if they were the only two on the court.

Swoosh! Swoosh!

She's good, Ava thought.

"Pair up for passing!" called Coach Rader.

"Hey, Tama—" Ava started. But Tamara spun away and paired up with Callie Wagner. Ava paired up with Madison Jackson, one of the other seventh graders.

Run, pass, run, pass. Ava kept her eyes trained on the ball. *You can't catch what you can't see,* her dad always said.

Suddenly the heavy gym door slammed open, and a tall, muscular boy bounded in. Ava swiveled her head in amazement and missed the catch.

"Sorry!" she called to Madison, and scurried after the ball. She watched the boy for a moment as he took his place next to Coach Rader. He had dark-blond hair and prominent cheekbones. His brown eyes drooped downward, giving him a sleepy look.

"What's *he* doing here?" Ava whispered to Madison.

"PJ Kelly? He's going to start volunteering after football workouts," Madison said. "He's our new assistant coach."

"Really?" Ava wasn't sure what to make of this. Why was the star high school quarterback bothering with the middle school girls' basketball team?

"Are you going to pass?" Madison asked. They were the only two not in motion.

"Yeah, sure." Ava threw the ball.

"Scrimmage!" Coach Rader quickly divided the girls into two groups, with Ava on the team with orange practice jerseys, and Tamara on the royal-blue team.

Ava immediately gained possession of the ball. She ran up court. But Tamara loomed large. She blocked Ava's throw, causing her shot to bounce off the rim.

"Excellent D!" called PJ, clearly pleased with Tamara's defensive moves.

Ava tore after her on the rebound, using her shoulder to knock the ball from Tamara.

"Hey, Ava! Not so rough!" called Coach Rader.

Ava made a mental note to tone it down. This wasn't football. People here didn't wear pads or expect to be tackled.

Ava dribbled around Jane Lopez, and then Tamara was on her again, stealing the ball.

Despite Ava's blocking, Tamara hit the three-pointer from the corner.

"Way to go, Tam!" PJ bellowed.

Madison passed the ball to Ava. Ava passed it to Callie, who sent it back into Ava's hands. Her heart pumped as she dribbled sloppily around Jane once again.

"Control! Control the ball!" PJ's deep voice rose above the pounding on the floorboards.

Does he know I'm Coach Sackett's daughter? Ava wondered. Probably. The whole town knew she and Alex were Coach Sackett's twin daughters. Suddenly Ava wanted to show him what she could do. She wanted to prove that she did have the "Sackett magic."

This called for her killer layup. When she played with her friend Jack Valdeavano in the park, he dubbed it her secret weapon.

No more holding back. Time to shine! Ava thought.

She broke for the basket. Tamara blocked her path. Ava faked right, then dodged left. Tamara stuck with her.

"Here! Over here, Ava!" cried Jane. Jane was wide open.

Ava knew she should pass. Tamara was taller and bigger, and left her no clear path. But she desperately wanted to show PJ her layup.

"Ava!" Jane called again.

Ava hesitated, and in that moment, Tamara swiped the ball from her. Ava watched in disbelief as Tamara executed a perfect layup. *Her* layup.

"You rock, Tam!" cheered PJ. Even Coach Rader clapped.

Ava felt the air seep out of her. On the football field, she was special because she was the only girl—and because she was better than a lot of the boys. She'd thought that on an all-girls' team, she'd automatically be the star. Now she saw that she wasn't.

"I'm out of practice," she announced suddenly. But no one answered.

The scrimmage started up again, and Ava got back into the game.

Maybe not today, but before the season ends, she vowed, *I'll show them that I'm as good as Tamara—maybe even better.*

CHAPTER TWO

"Wait up!" Alex called to Ava the next afternoon. Her sister didn't usually walk so fast. Ever since they were toddlers, Ava had been the one who had to keep up with Alex—their mom said Alex walked with a purpose.

"I'm sweaty," Ava complained, slowing down on the sidewalk outside their house. "I want to get inside and take a shower."

"Was practice rough?" Alex asked. They'd both taken the late bus home from school. Ava had stayed after for basketball practice, and Alex had stayed for a student council meeting.

Ava shrugged. "I'm out of shape."

"You?" Alex laughed. Somehow all the sporty

genes had gone to Ava. Her twin was the most athletic girl she knew.

At that moment, their dad's car pulled into the driveway. Tommy, the twins' older brother, burst out of the passenger side and sprinted for the front door. "First shower!" he called.

"No way!" Ava cried. She dashed up the front walk and struggled with her key in the lock.

"Move it, squirt." Tommy reached for the handle. "I quarterbacked all practice. I need that shower."

"Back off!" Ava cried. "Why'd you QB?"

"PJ never showed up." Tommy tried to push around her.

"Well, he wasn't at our practice," Ava said as she pushed back.

Alex watched her sweaty brother and sister jostle their way inside to fight for the hot water. Tommy had just come from high school football practice with Coach. He must have been tired because he let Ava shoot past him into the house. Alex was the only one who looked fresh in her black leggings and green-and-violet-striped shirt with her matching green headband.

"Hey there, pumpkin!" Coach Sackett pushed

his baseball cap back and walked toward the door. "How was your day?"

"Good, but I'm starving," Alex said. "I ate my lunch early so I could help Ms. Palmer organize the student council raffle during my lunch hour." When Ms. Palmer had asked for her help, Alex had hesitated. Not because she'd miss eating, but because she'd miss the chance to sit with Corey. She wanted to talk more about their date—and exactly when they would go out. It was the only thing she could think about all day. But how could she say no to Ms. Palmer as seventh-grade class president?

"Food. Right." Coach stepped inside and greeted their dog, Moxy, who ran in excited circles. Moxy was an Australian shepherd, and she almost never ran out of energy.

As she followed her dad into the kitchen, Alex's eyes swept the family room. Random pieces of clothing, magazines, dog toys, and popcorn crumbs littered the sofa. Dirty break-fast dishes lay on the kitchen table. An opened carton of milk had been out on the counter all day. Stray cornflakes crunched under her feet on the tile floor.

"Your mom would not be too happy about

all this." Coach began to collect the dirty dishes and dump them into the sink, which was already overflowing with pots and pans.

"You think?" Alex teased. Her mom had left yesterday morning to go to an artist retreat in the Texas hills. Ever since her ceramics business had taken off, she'd been dying to go to this special place with a fancy ceramics studio to work on her more complicated designs. The official football season was done, and Coach Sackett had convinced his wife that this week was a great time to go and he had everything at home under control.

"A rough beginning, I know." He filled the sink with water and soap bubbles. "We just need teamwork. You straighten the family room. I've got the kitchen."

"What about dinner?" Alex asked, grabbing an apple.

"Go for the first down, *then* you try for the end zone." Coach Sackett often spoke as if he were in the football locker room.

Alex guessed dinner would take a while. She checked her phone as she cleaned, hoping Corey would text. Should she text him? No, that would be weird, she decided. They'd never texted before. But maybe now was different.

"Moxy needs to go out!" Ava hurried down the stairs. Her wet hair was uncombed, and she wore a football jersey and flannel pants. Moxy scampered anxiously at her heels.

"Why don't you both take Moxy for a walk?" Mr. Sackett suggested. He came out of the kitchen holding Moxy's leash in one hand and a frozen chicken in the other. "I need to defrost this. The banana muffins I baked this morning won't do double duty for dinner."

"We better make it a *long* walk, Ave," Alex joked. "The pizza delivery guy takes a while." Coach was a great baker, but unfortunately not nearly as good of a cook as their mother.

"Do not doubt your dad. Somehow, someway, I am cooking chicken." He clipped the leash on Moxy. "Ava, your hair is wet. Put a coat on."

"But it feels like spring," Ava protested.

"No buts." Coach Sackett handed Alex the leash. "A coat, and stay only on our street. Promise?"

"Promise," the girls agreed.

Alex grabbed her new plaid peacoat from the front closet, while Ava pulled on the navy Windbreaker she'd worn last spring.

"Did this shrink?" Ava demanded. The jacket's sleeves ended just below Ava's elbows, and the fabric strained tightly across her back.

Alex doubled over in laughter. "You look ridiculous, Ave!"

"You grew a lot," Coach said. "Wear another jacket."

"I don't have another one." Ava pulled the navy one off. "Just my winter coat."

"That's because you always refuse to go shopping. Mom wanted to take you." Alex *never* refused a mall run.

Moxy let out a series of short, high yelps.

"I have an extra." Alex pulled out her cute hot-pink jacket with a trendy shawl collar. "You can wear this one."

"Seriously?" Ava rolled her eyes. "Never! That's so pink and so not me."

"Just throw it on." Coach sighed. "Help me here, Ava. Moxy needs to go pronto, and I need to make dinner."

Ava echoed his sigh, reluctantly slipping on the hot-pink jacket. They hurried Moxy outside.

"Hey," Alex called to Ava, who had already been pulled ahead by Moxy as they headed down their block. "You look like me."

"Didn't anyone ever tell you? We're twins," Ava called back.

"Obviously! I mean from the back, with the pink coat. Plus, your hair has grown out a lot," Alex explained.

Ava touched the ends of her wet, tangled hair. They now grazed her shoulders. "I need a haircut."

When they'd first moved to Ashland, Ava had cut her hair just below her chin without consulting Alex. At the time, it had felt like a betrayal to Alex. They'd always had different interests, but Alex took comfort in looking exactly the same as Ava. Now that they were no longer the "new girls," she knew it would take a whole lot more than a haircut to weaken their twin bond.

Alex and Ava walked side by side with Moxy on the leash between them. The air was warmer than it had been in months, although it had never gotten anywhere as cold as it used to in Boston during the winters. It had snowed only once, and that was just flurries!

"Time to turn around," Ava said when they reach the end of their street.

"Let's keep walking. I have something amazing to tell you," Alex said.

"But we promised—" Ava started.

"I know, but it's so nice out, and Coach will need forever to try to cook that frozen chicken. We'll just walk down Ridgewood. It's no big deal." Alex grabbed Moxy's leash and headed right before Ava could protest. Then she called over her shoulder. "Corey asked me out."

Ava raced after her. "What?"

"You heard me," Alex said breezily, as if it weren't the big deal that it clearly was.

"When? How? I need details!" Ava cried.

As they walked down Ridgewood, then turned onto Quincy Street, Alex told Ava everything she knew, which she soon realized wasn't much.

"Does this mean you guys are a couple?" Ava asked

"I don't know," Alex admitted.

"So is it just the two of you at the movies? Are other people going?" Ava asked.

"No clue," Alex admitted. "Do you think other people should go too?"

"Definitely. Especially if you have this all wrong and he thinks you're going to the movies as friends," Ava said.

"Why would he think that?" Alex demanded.

"I've gone to the movies with Corey, Xander,

and Kal, and I am sure not going out with any of them," Ava said.

"That's different," Alex said, as they turned onto another street. "You went to the movies as a football team."

"All I'm saying is we never go to a restaurant without you pulling up the menu online, analyzing every option, and knowing what you're going to order before we even get there. It just seems odd to me that you don't know what kind of date this is or if it is a date," Ava said.

Alex slowed. Ava was right. How could she not know all this?

She loosened her grip on the leash and fumbled in her coat pocket for her phone. It didn't seem to be there. She must've left it in the house. "Ugh, I need to text Emily—" Alex let out a shriek as a rabbit jumped out from a nearby bush and Moxy lunged after it, yanking the leash from her hand. With it flapping on the pavement behind her, Moxy raced down the street after the rabbit.

"Moxy! Stop!" Alex screamed.

But Moxy kept moving at top speed, intent on catching the rabbit.

"Come back!" Alex cried, as she and Ava started to run too. Moxy cut through lawn after lawn and zigzagged down unfamiliar streets. They chased her across backyards until she disappeared behind a cluster of trees.

Alex ran as fast as she could, gasping for breath. "Where is she?"

"There!" Ava cried. She pointed, and Alex glimpsed Moxy heading for a street behind the trees. She heard a car horn beep.

"Oh no!" Alex cried.

Ava's body reacted to the car horn as if it were the starting gun at a race. Leaving Alex far behind, she burst forward and sprinted faster than she'd ever run on the football field.

Moxy! She had to get to Moxy before . . .

She spotted Moxy on a lawn, momentarily startled by the noise. Her dog stood, panting, alongside the curb. The rabbit was long gone. Ava didn't bother to yell. She flung her body and tackled Moxy from behind, grabbing her collar with her hands. Moxy squirmed, but Ava held on tightly, rolling over in the grass.

"Hey, girl, hey, girl," she repeated. "I've got you."

Alex reached them and grabbed the leash.

Then she waved to the woman in the stopped car. "Thanks so much! Sorry 'bout that!" The woman cautioned them to be careful, then drove off.

Ava stayed on the ground curled around Moxy, catching her breath. "I'm glad I was wearing sneakers."

"You saved her." Alex sat with them.

Ava looked around. "Where are we?"

"Someone's yard?" Alex gazed around, disoriented. "I don't recognize these houses."

"Me neither." Ava stood and whirled about. "Should we call Coach to come get us?" Ava asked.

"I don't have my phone, remember? Besides, if we called him, we'd get in trouble. We promised we wouldn't leave our block. We just need to retrace our steps," Alex said. "I think we should cut through this yard. I'm pretty sure we came from the street behind this house." She led them up a narrow driveway. A row of thick, high hedges bordered the backyard.

"Are you sure?" Ava asked. She'd never been great at directions. "Look, here comes someone. Maybe we should ask." She pointed to a light-blue truck driving down the street.

"No way. I'm not talking to some stranger.

29

I've got this," Alex assured her. The truck slowed in front of the house and began to turn up the driveway. "They must live here. Hide!"

"What? Why?" Ava asked, bewildered.

"Quick!" Alex pulled her and Moxy behind the tall hedge.

"This is silly. We can run across the lawn. They won't see us. And if they do, they don't know us." Ava pointed out the path they would take. The truck had pulled to the top of the drive-way. Only the hedge separated them. "Ready? Okay—" Then she spotted the man stepping out of the driver's side. Ava stared in disbelief. It was Mr. Kelly! He walked around the back of the truck. She knew the Kellys lived in their neighborhood, but how was it possible that she and Alex had ended up at *their* house?

"Wait!" She grabbed Alex's arm to stop her. Ava squeezed her other hand around Moxy's snout to keep the dog quiet.

Mr. Kelly would surely recognize the Sackett twins. How would they explain why they were in his backyard? He hated Coach already and loved making trouble for their family. It was less risky to hide behind the thick leaves until he went inside.

She caught Alex's eye. Ava could tell her twin knew exactly what she was thinking.

Ava held Moxy tightly and watched through gaps in the leaves as Mr. Kelly opened the passenger door. PJ Kelly hobbled out. Ava held back her gasp. Coach's star quarterback was injured! PJ's left knee was cased in a big black brace, and he leaned heavily on crutches. Dried mud covered his track pants and arms. A large bruise bloomed on his left cheek. Even from where she hid, Ava could see him cringe in pain.

Alex nudged her and raised her eyebrows in alarm. "What happened?" she mouthed silently.

Ava raised her eyebrows back. She remembered that Tommy said PJ hadn't been at practice today. And he hadn't been at her basketball practice either. So what had happened? Did Coach know?

"I didn't like that doctor," PJ said to his dad. "Dr. Rodriguez is much nicer."

"Do you think I wanted to take off work and drive you five towns away to Hellman? You're lucky I got Dr. Chang to see you at all. And that he promised to keep his mouth shut," Mr. Kelly grumbled. "Dr. Rodriguez's office is crawling with folks from Ashland. Coach Sackett would already know what you've been up to if I were stupid enough to take you to him."

Mr. Kelly moved around to the back of the pickup. "Speaking of stupid . . ." Mr. Kelly lifted a mangled dirt bike from the truck's bed. "What would possibly possess you to go dirt biking by that quarry?"

"You said you wanted me to bond with the guys from Saint Francis," PJ replied.

"Bond, yeah. Have a burger. Watch some movies. Not twist your knee so you're benched from football!" Mr. Kelly yelled.

"I wasn't trying to do that," PJ shot back. "We'd had a great practice, and they were all going, so it seemed like the right thing."

"You're just not getting it. They want your skill and talent. That's why they invited you to their football practice. Their quarterback is graduating," Mr. Kelly said. "They need you. You have nothing to prove to them."

PJ leaned against the truck. "I don't get why leaving Ashland High is a good thing. It feels wrong. I mean, we just won state."

"Look at the big picture, son. Saint Francis is a private school with a lot of money to spend on football. They are putting together a super team of the best players in the state, and *you* will be the face of that team. The men behind this team—the men with money and power— will get you into the college of your dreams, and then they will get you into the NFL." Mr. Kelly beamed. "Boom! Just like that."

"But Coach Sackett—" PJ started.

"Coach Sackett is small-time. Outside Ashland, he has no connections and no power. Saint Francis is your ticket to the big leagues." Mr. Kelly opened the garage door and tossed the mangled bike inside. "*No one* can know about this. The dirt biking or the Saint Francis practice."

"Coach Sackett is not going to be happy that I'm injured," PJ said.

"No one is happy, believe me. Now go put some ice on that knee. That knee is your future!" Mr. Kelly stalked into the garage.

As PJ began to hobble after him, Moxy wriggled her mouth free and let out a strained yelp of frustration.

PJ stopped. He looked over his shoulder and squinted in their direction.

Ava heard her own heart pound. She clamped her hands tighter over Moxy's mouth. Had PJ seen them?

CHAPTER THREE

Go away, go away, Alex chanted silently, trying to motivate PJ with the power of her mind.

PJ's eyes scanned the yard as he balanced on his crutches. Alex, Ava, and even Moxy froze.

Go away.

PJ turned and slowly made his way into the house. Mind-power triumph!

"I was sure he saw us. I thought I was going to have a heart attack." Alex exhaled loudly.

"Me too. Let's get out of here." Ava tightened her grip on Moxy's leash and ran across the yard.

"I'm pretty sure I know the way," said Alex. She led them in and out of a few yards until she found Quincy Street again. They slowed to a walk and caught their breath. "Okay, what just happened back there? Is PJ really ditching the Tigers?"

"He's such a traitor!" Ava cried.

"He's stupid, too. Daddy told his players not to do dangerous things like dirt biking. He's going to be mad," Alex said.

"He's going to be *furious*. And not only about the injury, but about PJ and his dad being dirty, rotten, sneaky liars!" Ava's face grew red. "I can't wait to tell Coach."

"Whoa!" Alex grabbed Ava's shoulder. "I don't think we should."

"What? Why not?" Ava demanded.

Alex chewed her lip. "We did something that we weren't supposed to do too. We promised that we wouldn't leave the block."

"That's different," Ava scoffed.

"I don't know. Dad hates it when we break the rules. He might punish us. He might not let me go to the movies with Corey." Alex suddenly wished she had listened. No movies might mean no boyfriend and then no kiss. She couldn't cancel on Corey *again*—she'd already had to do that once when he'd asked her to hang out at the park. She didn't think that was a date, but she never got to find out, because she had to study with Max, a boy in her social studies class she was helping. If she bailed on Corey again, she was sure he wouldn't ask her out a third time.

"News flash, Alex. This is not about you. It's about the team—and PJ," Ava said, as they neared home.

"But you don't know that PJ is really going to leave. He sounded unsure to me. In fact, he sounded like he didn't want to go," Alex pointed out.

"Mr. Kelly sounded sure," Ava retorted.

"But that's not the same. I don't think we should rat PJ out. We should give him the chance to talk to Dad tomorrow. I bet he'll come to practice and fess up about it," Alex insisted.

"I don't know." Ava kicked a stone, and they watched it skitter down the street.

"It's not our secret to tell. And we were eavesdropping, which is dishonest," Alex added.

"Is this about honesty or you going out with Corey?" Ava asked.

"Both." Alex locked eyes with her twin. "Please, Ave? I don't want to get in trouble. I know I said we should keep walking, and I dropped the leash. I'm sorry."

"But—"

Alex didn't let her finish. "Whatever happens with PJ is going to happen whether Daddy finds out tonight or tomorrow. And I don't want him to have to tell Mr. Kelly he knows because his daughters were spying on him in his own yard. That would be bad."

Ava nodded thoughtfully. "Yeah, that would be bad. Okay, I'll keep the secret."

"Thanks." Alex hugged Ava and pushed open their front door. "Oh, it smells good!"

"Spaghetti!" Coach called from the kitchen. "Tommy's waiting. Let's eat!"

"What happened to Mr. Chicken?" Alex teased after they'd all sat at the table. She was glad he'd gone with spaghetti. She'd given up eating meat, and if they were all eating chicken, she'd be left with just salad. She was also relieved that cooking had distracted her dad from how long they'd been gone. Their mom would have been all over them.

"He's still icing his injuries," Coach joked. "Mr. Chicken is benched for now. He'll play in a game later this week."

"Sounds like Mr. Chicken belongs on our team." Tommy's cheeks bulged with pasta.

"What's that mean?" Ava asked.

Coach shook his head. "We're down a lot of guys. Dion's still recovering from his concussion in the play-offs. Winston tore his Achilles so he's out, and Derek has mono. And then there are the Zhou and the Whitley families. They're running scared."

"From you?" Alex joked.

Her dad didn't laugh. "No—from football. They don't want their sons to play, because they fear the long-term effects. Concussions and brain damage." He sighed. "It's hard to argue with that. I run safe practices. I teach the guys how to take a hit, but I can't guarantee an injury won't occur."

"Don't sweat it. It's only the spring season, and these practice games don't count for much," Tommy offered.

"True. By next fall, everyone will be healthy and strong and ready to play. Plus, all my core players are returning—PJ, Dion, and Tyler," Coach added. "Nothing to worry about."

Alex felt the heat of Ava's accusing gaze, but she refused to look in her sister's direction. She was not telling him about PJ now. *No way.* She wished they'd never overheard that conversation.

She crossed her fingers under the table and hoped that PJ would do the right thing and stay with the Tigers.

Ava slumped on the bench during halftime at the next evening's game, only partially listening to Coach Rader's speech. The basketball team lagged behind, and Ava was totally off her game. She'd been missing opportunities—her shots pulled left, and her moves felt timid.

Get in the game, Sackett! Focus! She tried to give herself her own pep talk.

She knew she could play better. The whole first half she'd been too aware of Jack, Xander, and Kal up in the stands, not to mention the loud woman calling directions to Tamara. She glanced over at Tamara, confidently doing calf stretches. Tamara had outscored her.

"Where's PJ?" Whitney LaVersa asked Jane in a whisper. "I bet his halftime talks are better."

"No idea. He bailed on us." Jane shrugged.

Had PJ gone to football practice this afternoon and confessed? Ava wondered. That couldn't have gone well. Maybe that was why he'd missed their game. Jane's mom had driven her to practice, so she hadn't seen her dad or Tommy yet today.

"Go, Tiger Cubs! Play tough!" yelled the woman in the stands, as Ava and her team hit the court again.

"Who's that?" she asked Madison as they took their positions.

"Tamara's mom." Madison rolled her eyes. "Can't miss her."

Ava's mom was still at her artist retreat and her dad was coaching at the high school tonight, but when they did come to her games, Ava was grateful that they mostly kept quiet. Mrs. Baker was mortifyingly loud.

The whistle blew, and Ava quickly gained possession and swished the ball through the net. Now a tall girl with dozens of skinny braids from the other team had the ball. Ava tried to block her. She moved right, and Ava followed. She moved left, and Ava tried to trip her up. Her fingertips brushed the ball.

"Go, Tam! Get in her face!" Mrs. Baker's shrill voice yelled from the stands.

Tamara raced over, and the girl passed the ball to a teammate across the court. Ava gritted her teeth. She could've stolen the ball if Tamara hadn't gotten in the way.

Tamara was all over the next girl too. Her mother screamed directions to her. Tamara scored again and again.

"You rule, Tam! Show them what you got!" Mrs. Baker cheered.

Ava caught a pass from Jane and turned to send it to Callie when the girl with the braids blocked her path.

"On her, Tam!" Mrs. Baker yelled.

Out of the corner of her eye, Ava saw Tamara move toward them.

Oh, no you don't, Ava thought. She wished she weren't so competitive, but she was. She wanted to show Tamara, and her screaming mother, and all the football boys in the stands that she had better skills.

Ava barreled into the braided girl, knocking the ball from her possession. Scooping up the ball, Ava dribbled for the basket until the referee's shrill whistle stopped her.

He called a foul: unnecessary roughness. A few minutes later, she was called out again.

"It's not football, Ava," Coach Rader scolded her.

"I know," Ava said, frustrated, as the clock ran down and they lost the game. She hated to lose her first game of the season. The opposing team hadn't been all that great. They should have beaten them.

Ava pulled on her warm-up jacket and turned to high-five the other team.

"That Sackett girl totally messed up the team rhythm." Mrs. Baker's loud voice carried down from the stands. "We won before she showed up."

Ava willed herself not to turn and acknowledge what she'd heard. She was a great athlete, she knew that. Losing couldn't be her fault. Could it?

CHAPTER FOUR

"So here's the plan," Emily said on Thursday afternoon. "Next Friday, after the movie, we come back here to my house."

"I'm so excited!" Alex tucked her legs under her on the sofa and reached for another chip. It had been decided. In one week, she, Corey, Emily, Greg, Lindsey, and Johnny were all going to the movies together.

"A party!" Lindsey cried.

"No. Not really. Just the six of us," Emily cautioned. "And maybe Rosa and Ryan, too. How amazing is it that practically our whole group now has boyfriends?"

"Very." Alex couldn't believe that she was finally included.

"Are you and Corey officially going out?" Lindsey leaned toward Alex.

Alex paused before she dipped another chip into salsa. Was this a trick question? She knew Lindsey was going out with Johnny now, but she and Corey did have a long history. And Lindsey certainly could hold a grudge—Alex thought about how mean she'd recently been to Max, just because he'd teased Lindsey about using a word incorrectly.

"Well, not yet, exactly, but . . . ," she fumbled to respond.

"You should be. You guys are so cute together," Lindsey said. "I mean it. Truly."

"Corey asked me if you like him," Emily added.

"Really?" Alex hesitated. "What did you say?"

"Mr. Loffit was handing out the quiz and made us stop talking, so I didn't get to answer," Emily confided. "But I think not answering gives you a bit of mystery."

"Is that a good thing?" Alex kind of wished Emily had said yes. She didn't think she'd ever have the nerve to tell Corey herself that she liked him.

"Totally." Lindsey shot her a genuine smile. "It's better this way. Now, let's talk clothes. I vote you should wear your blue sweater with the white sleeves. I like that one."

Alex spent the next hour planning every part of the movie date with Emily and Lindsey. Her clothes: blue sweater, gray jeans. Snacks to buy: share popcorn and sour gummies. Where to sit: Lindsey promised to sit on the opposite end of the row from Alex and Corey.

This was going to be the best night of her life. Alex just wanted it to happen already!

That evening at the dinner table, Alex wondered if she should tell her dad that she had plans to go out next Friday night. She definitely didn't want to tell him the boyfriend or date part. She'd wait for her mom for that. But she couldn't find the right time. He was in a grumpy mood. PJ had told him that he was injured. As far as Alex could figure, PJ hadn't told him how the injury happened or that he'd been with the Saint Francis team.

"Your cooking stinks, Alex." Tommy pulled slightly burnt crusts from his grilled cheese sandwich.

"Hey! My grilled cheese and tomato soup are

far superior to anything you will make tomorrow," Alex shot back. They had divided up the cooking responsibilities for the rest of the time Mrs. Sackett was away.

"Chef Tommy has hidden cooking talents that you know nothing about," Tommy promised.

"Ever think there's a reason these talents have been hidden for sixteen years?" Ava teased.

"Do not doubt me," Tommy said. "My meal will be epic and gourmet."

"If you have such mad skills, maybe you should cook a romantic meal for Cassie on her birthday," Ava suggested with a mischievous grin.

"It took Tommy long enough to get Cassie to go out with him," Coach Sackett teased. "Let's not poison his girlfriend just yet."

Tommy clasped his hands over his heart. "I am wounded by you nonbelievers."

"So you think that cooking for Cassie's birthday is a stellar idea?" Alex asked.

Tommy sighed. "Not at all. And I have no idea what to get her."

"How about a Tigers jersey with your number on it?" Ava suggested. "Or a football that you sign for her?"

"No! That's not something *she* would want. Why does she want to wear his jersey?" Alex asked. "He should get her something pretty and romantic."

"Like a heart necklace?" Tommy asked hopefully.

"That's so typical," Ava scoffed. "The gift needs to be more personal. How about you write her a song?"

"Oh, I like that! A love ballad. And he can sing it to her at school." Alex pictured Tommy with his keyboard, singing to Cassie. Tommy was a great musician.

Tommy's eyes went wide. "I can't write that kind of thing. And I'm sure not singing to her in front of everyone."

"What about a candle?" Coach offered. "You know, one of those smelly candles they sell in the mall. Don't girls like those?"

Alex groaned. "You get a candle for your teacher at Christmas. A boyfriend has to do something much more romantic."

"You're suddenly a boyfriend expert?" Her father raised his eyebrows and grinned.

"Actually, she kind of is—" Ava began as the phone rang, and their dad stood to answer it.

"Don't say anything," Alex whispered to Ava.

"About what?" Tommy asked.

"Nothing." Alex didn't want to talk to her dad or Tommy about Corey right now. Besides, there was nothing to talk about . . . yet.

"Yes, of course, I'm familiar with TexasHigh-Sports.com. Everyone reads the daily blogs," Coach said to the person on the other end of the phone and motioned for the kids to clear the table.

Alex brought her plate to the sink and listened to her dad answer questions about his team's prospects for the next season.

"Yes, we do have injuries. All teams experience this kind of thing," Coach Sackett said as he held up a grilled cheese crust. Moxy jumped for it.

"Ava, go long to the fridge," Tommy commanded.

Alex groaned. Her brother and sister never stopped playing football—even when they didn't even have a football. Tommy tossed the ketchup bottle to Ava. She caught it and did a victory dance.

"Mom would make you stop," Alex reminded them.

"Mom's not here." Tommy quarterbacked a

box of soup crackers. Ava caught it and lapped the kitchen. Tommy cheered.

"No, I'm not concerned about PJ Kelly being out. The boy will heal." Coach dodged out of Ava's path and held up more crusts for Moxy. Moxy barked in anticipation. "What? Too much conditioning? Who said that?"

"Catch, Ave!" Tommy called. He hurled a small jar of pickles her way.

"I do not over-condition my players! Whoa!" Coach cried, and the jar slipped from Ava's grip and crashed to the floor. Pickle juice and shards of glass flew everywhere. Moxy ran to investigate. "Get the dog away! What? No, I wasn't talking to you."

Alex grabbed Moxy by her collar. Tommy found the garbage can and a dish towel.

"Sorry? What were you saying?" Coach tucked the phone under his shoulder and began to pick pieces of glass from the spreading puddle. "Look, injured football players are not a big deal. It happens all the time. There's really no story here." Moxy barked and lunged for the stray pickles. "Alex, get her!"

Alex grabbed Moxy by the collar, but not before the dog slid through the puddle. Moxy gave a shake, spraying pickle juice in her dad's eyes.

"Do I have anything else to say?" Coach sputtered, wiping his face with his sleeve. "No. Listen, can we talk another time?"

After they'd cleaned the mess, Alex hurried upstairs to her bedroom. She opened her jewelry box and surveyed its contents. What necklace would look best with the blue sweater? She liked the gold one with the bicycle charm.

"Hey." Ava pushed open her door and flopped onto her bed. "I think we should tell him."

"Tell who what?" Alex held up a necklace with a silver *A* pendent. "This isn't bad."

"Tell Coach about PJ." Ava tossed Poppet, Alex's pale-pink stuffed bunny, up into the air as she spoke. "Or tell someone. Tell Tommy."

"Why?" Alex grabbed for her bunny.

"Because PJ lied. He told Coach that he got hurt from too many conditioning drills at practice. He's making it sound like his knee injury is Coach's fault," Ava said.

"But if we tell Tommy, he's going to tell Dad. He'll be angry that we disobeyed him and left our street." Alex shook her head. "We talked about this. It's better for everyone if we don't say anything."

"It's better for you," Ava said.

"You too. You don't want to get grounded," Alex pointed out. "What if they make you stop playing basketball?"

Ava was quiet for a minute. "But I don't want the Tigers all messed up," she said.

"PJ is out no matter how he got injured. Nothing we say is going to change that, and we don't know for sure what he's going to do with the team. We should stay out of it, and every-thing will be fine," Alex assured her.

"You don't know that," Ava protested.

"Don't you have other things to worry about besides the high school team?" Alex asked, exas-perated.

"What's that supposed to mean?" Ava shot back.

Alex was worried about her date with Corey— how to make it fabulous so he would want to go out again. She didn't want to worry about PJ and the high school team. "Nothing. Forget it."

"Maybe I will and maybe I won't." Ava stood and walked to the door.

"You promised, Ave," Alex reminded her. "A twin promise."

When they were in kindergarten, they had

made a rule that a twin promise was the most special kind of promise. Alex knew that even if Ava was angry, she'd never break a twin promise.

"You're getting it, Ava!" Luke Grabowski grinned the next afternoon when Ava circled the correct pronoun on her English homework.

"Yeah, I guess." Ava held back her own grin, but she was proud of herself. Grammar worksheets always tripped her up. "Can you come to school with me and squat down next to my desk? It's easier with you next to me."

"Sounds painful. Besides, I don't think the middle school wants me crouching by your desk all day." Luke snorted. He was a sophomore at Ashland High and nearing six feet tall. "Hey, you can do this without me."

"I'm not so sure." Ever since Luke had started tutoring her this year, Ava's grades had improved. And everything just made more sense. But sometimes in the classroom, her mind started to wander and she couldn't focus on the test or worksheet. She knew this was part of her ADHD diagnosis, but having it labeled didn't always make it easier. "It's like with sports. I like the whole team thing with football and basketball. I can't imagine being an ice skater or a swimmer and having to go out on my own. I'd totally get off track."

"Okay, think of me as your imaginary teammate. When you get off track, pretend I am squatting next to you and hear my voice in your head saying—"

"I'm starving!" Tommy announced, bursting into the kitchen.

"Not that," Luke said. "Something more inspiring."

"Food inspires *me*." Tommy opened the refrigerator and grimaced. "Mom has been gone for five whole days. I think I may starve to death."

"You are not going to starve to death!" Coach followed Tommy inside after football practice. "Do not tell your mother I haven't been feeding you."

"Then please feed me," Tommy joked.

"I thought it was your night to cook," Ava reminded him.

Tommy groaned. "With what? It's like an episode of a cooking reality show in here. How can I make my gourmet dinner with the random ingredients we have?"

"What do you suggest?" Coach asked, sinking into a chair. He looked tired.

"I suggest that I go to the mall and find Cassie a birthday present and swing by the food court and grab burgers for everyone." Tommy closed the fridge. "Want to take a ride, Luke?"

"Sure thing." Luke stood.

"Can I come too?" Ava asked. "I can eat my burger at the mall while you shop and then you can drop me off at basketball. We have a night practice at the gym, and I already changed my clothes." She stood and grabbed her bag. "Oh, Alex is at Emily's house again, but she's coming back soon," she told Coach.

"Sounds like a plan." Coach closed his eyes. "It's still chilly out. Ava, wear a coat."

"What's with the coat? Mom never makes me wear a coat," Ava grumbled.

"Aha!" Coach brightened. "You be sure to tell her that I kept you very warm this week."

"Warm and hungry!" Tommy called over his shoulder, as Ava grabbed Alex's pink coat off the back of a chair and followed him and Luke to the car.

"So what are you getting Cassie?" Ava asked as they entered the mall. The food court bustled with Friday evening crowds. She recognized the Fowler twins and a group of kids from school by the waffle fry place.

Tommy pushed his hands deep into his pockets and shrugged. "I have an idea."

"Spill it," Luke encouraged. "This'll be good."

"It's not fully formed yet." The tips of Tommy's ears reddened with embarrassment.

"Come on—"

"Hey, Luke, will you take me to get my burger?" Ava jumped in, hoping to help Tommy. He was new to this boyfriend business—and Luke constantly ribbed him. She sensed Tommy needed space to shop. "I need to eat before practice."

Ava and Luke found a table in the food court and ordered cheeseburgers and fries. As she shoved the change the cashier handed her into the pocket of her coat, her fingertips landed on one of Alex's stretchy pink headbands. She pulled it on, pushing her overgrown hair out of her eyes, as Luke asked her about basketball.

"There are only three more games left this season." Ava chewed thoughtfully. "I was thinking that I might sit them out."

"Why would you do that?" Luke leaned

forward. Ava liked how he listened to her. Tommy never listened like Luke did.

Ava told him about how off her first game back had been and how out of sync with the team she felt. "I'm messing them up. They did better without me."

"Isn't that the coach's decision to make? If he doesn't want to play you, he doesn't have to. Besides, no one blames just you for that loss," Luke assured her.

But Ava knew Mrs. Baker blamed her. Maybe others, too.

"Do you like playing?" he asked.

"Yes, but—"

"No buts. It's a simple question," Luke said.

"Not really. I stink right now." Ava pushed away her fries, no longer hungry. "I wonder if I came back too soon. Maybe I need more time to work on my skills."

And to get better than Tamara, she thought.

She felt guilty. Since her Pee Wee team days, Coach Sackett had reminded her endlessly that sports weren't about being the best on the team. But being second to Tamara bothered her.

"So do I stay with the team? Quick! Yes or no?" Ava asked Luke.

"I can't decide that for you," Luke protested.

"How do I decide?" Ava asked.

"I think you need to play in another game and see how you feel." Then Luke grinned mischievously. "Or you can ask Mr. Wonder."

"Who?"

Luke tapped the screen of his phone. "Mr. Wonder. Have you seen this awesome app? It tells your future." Animation of a funny little guy with big ears and a glowing blue crystal ball appeared. The character danced along what looked to be an oversize hand. "First you measure the lines on your palm."

Luke scooted his chair closer, reached for Ava's hand, and flipped it over. He traced the lines. "This is your line of good fortune. And this is your line of grit."

"Grit like dirt?" Ava giggled.

"No, grit like perseverance and determination." Luke followed the line with his finger. "Look how long it is!" He typed something into the app.

"What does Mr. Wonder say?' Ava asked.

"Mr. Wonder says you are not a quitter." Luke shot her a meaningful look. "And Mr. Wonder knows all."

CHAPTER FIVE

Five more days, Alex thought as she walked into the cafeteria on Monday. Her fingertips tingled just thinking about the group date on Friday. She was dying to see Corey and talk to him. Emily and Lindsey, too. She'd been out of the loop all weekend.

On Saturday morning Coach had dragged them to visit Uncle Scott in the remote ranching town of Eagle Ridge, about forty-five minutes from Ashland. Uncle Scott was her dad's younger brother. He'd lived with them for a while but had recently gotten a job as a software engineer and moved into his own apartment. Uncle Scott was starting a community garden, and he'd proudly brought them all to volunteer at a composting plant, which had been kind of cool, but also smelly and disgusting! Even Ava and Tommy thought so. Alex could see why her mom had encouraged them to visit while she was away.

She wondered if Corey had missed her. Had he even known she was away? *He must have,* she thought.

"Hi!" she called brightly as she approached their lunch table. She flipped her hair to the side the way girls on TV did. Her dark curls looked particularly shiny today, especially against her pale-pink shirt.

"Hey!" Emily called. Lindsey and Rosa greeted her too.

Alex tried to lock eyes with Corey, but his gaze stayed fixed on the block of mac-and-cheese on his tray. Kal sat next to Corey, but he pushed down, making room for Alex. She liked that everyone already thought of them as a couple.

Corey and Alex. Alex and Corey. Their names sounded so good together.

"How was your weekend?" she asked him, pulling a blueberry yogurt from her brown paper bag.

Corey shrugged.

Alex began to tell him about Eagle Ridge. How Uncle Scott had taken them on a long hike and showed them how to make a meal from weeds and wild berries. It had actually been pretty good.

After a few minutes, Alex realized that Corey hadn't said one word. Was she rambling? She had a tendency to do that. "Sorry I'm being really verbose today," she said.

"What?" Corey asked. "What does that mean?"

"You speak like you're in college, Alex!" Rosa said with a slight giggle.

"No, I don't," Alex protested.

"It's not a bad thing. Really." Emily had seen her panicked expression.

"We're probably too immature for you to hang with," Corey said in an oddly flat voice.

"No way! Come on!" She elbowed him playfully. "Hey, how's this for mature?" She balanced her plastic spoon on the tip of her nose. "Ta-da!"

"Let me try!" Kal said. Rosa and Emily tried too. Soon they were all laughing and snapping spoon-nose photos. Everyone except Corey. Instead he silently stabbed holes in his congealed pasta with his fork.

"Are you okay? Is something wrong?" Alex asked quietly.

"Fine." He wouldn't look at her.

Alex wasn't sure what to do. Corey was obviously having a bad day. For a few minutes, she ate her yogurt in perplexed silence and listened to the conversation swirl around them. Then she decided to try again.

"Did you see the *Ashland Times*?" When he didn't answer, Alex continued. "They reviewed *Escape from Dark Woods*. They said it was pee-in-your-pants scary."

As soon as the words were out, she regretted them. Peeing in your pants was not a very romantic image.

"I mean, not that I'm going to—or you—or any of us, really." Alex's stomach twisted, as if it were being squeezed. Why was Corey just sitting there, staring at his tray? He always joked around with her. That was one of the things she liked most about him.

She left him alone. Sometimes when she was in a bad mood, she just wanted to be in a bad mood and didn't want Ava trying to cheer her up. Instead she talked to Emily about the English test. The bell finally rang, and Alex hurried to the trash can so she could walk out with Emily. She was dying to see what her friend thought of Corey's moodiness.

"Alex." Corey appeared next to her.

"Hi." She grinned. He had snapped out of it already.

"I can't go to the movies on Friday."

"Okay," Alex said, relieved they were talking again. "Maybe Saturday then? Or I bet we could move it all to next week."

"Um . . ." He stared at his sneakers. "That won't work."

"The movies? We can do something else," she offered. She hadn't wanted to see a scary movie anyway.

"No. I don't think so. There's a lot going on right now, so it's just not . . . not going to happen." He took a large step back, then another, putting distance between them.

"Is this about Max?" Alex asked suddenly. Corey couldn't still be jealous, could he? She'd only been helping Max with social studies. "I don't like him like that."

"I know, you told me that. But you can do whatever you like, anyway . . . it's a free country." He crossed his arms and refused to meet her gaze.

Alex stared at him. Why was he talking about America being a free country? "So, are we—?"

"No. Look, I've got to, uh, get to class." He hurried out of the cafeteria and was swallowed up by the hallway crowds. Part of her wanted to chase after him and beg for an explanation. But the part of her that stayed frozen next to the trash can knew the horrible truth.

She had been dumped.

"You coming, Alex?" Emily waited for her with Lindsey and Rosa.

"No. I need to do something," Alex lied, struggling to hold back the tears. She wasn't ready to tell her friends—who all had boyfriends—that she been dumped *before* her first date.

Ava burned up the court on Monday afternoon in the game against the Plainview Pioneers. The Plainview girls played hard. Ava tried to play harder. She dodged the guards and hit the rim from the outside. Then she sank a three-pointer. Mr. Wonder was right—she wasn't a quitter.

But Tamara was everywhere. Every basket Ava netted, Tamara netted two. Ava sprang up for a layup. Tamara jumped higher. Ava blocked. Tamara blocked harder.

"You show 'em, Tam!" Mrs. Baker yelled over and over from the stands.

"You're messing up our plays, Sackett," Tamara said under her breath as they set up again. "Hang back a bit, okay? I've got this."

Ava seethed. She didn't want to hang back. Why did Tamara think she was queen of the court?

"Teamwork, girls!" PJ Kelly called from the side. He leaned heavily on his crutches, tracking the game's progress.

Just hearing his voice made her angry. Her dad still knew nothing about his dirt bike accident and the Saint Francis super-team tryout.

Ava turned her focus back to the action on the court, but Plainview scored eight points in a row. The louder Mrs. Baker screamed and the more Tamara shone, the more frustrated Ava grew. She tried to get around the Plainview guard and found herself fouled once more for roughness.

Coach Rader called her out and sent Jane in. Ava sat on the bench and closed her eyes. Why had she done that?

"Hey, Little Sackett."

Ava opened her eyes to find PJ sitting next to her. His brown eyes searched hers, and he gave her a slight grin. "Tough time out there?"

Ava stiffened and looked away. She refused to talk to him.

"Doesn't look promising." He pointed to the scoreboard. Their team was down sixteen points with only three minutes left.

Ava stayed silent.

"You don't need to do that out there, you know," he said softly.

"Do what?" So much for her short-lived vow of silence.

"All that pushing and fouling. You have great skills. Let them shine. You don't need anything else," he said.

"Thanks." She folded her arms. She didn't want him to see that she appreciated his compliment.

"Just my opinion, but I think you've lost focus of who you're playing against out there."

"I know who I'm playing against," Ava retorted, annoyed again. He didn't know her.

"Do you? Sometimes you look as if you're playing against Tamara, your own teammate."

Ava cringed inwardly. PJ was right. Today's game had become about showing up Tamara. Why did that keep happening?

"Ride your talent, Little Sackett," PJ advised. "Play the game, don't let the game play you."

"Hey! That's one of Coach's sayings." She whirled to face him.

"I know." PJ grinned again. "I like borrowing them. Your dad has some great ones." PJ then reeled off a few of Coach's other favorites.

Ava found herself nodding. "I've been hearing them my whole life and I still like them."

"You're lucky," PJ said. "Your dad is truly great at what he does."

"Thanks. I think so too," Ava agreed. She was surprised that PJ felt this way. "Do you want to coach someday? Is that why you're coaching us?"

"I never really considered it, but yeah, maybe someday after I'm done playing and all that." PJ sighed. "It's scary to think that far ahead."

"You'd be a good coach." Ava couldn't believe she was being nice to PJ Kelly.

"Really? That means a lot coming from you," PJ said. "I guess it was a good thing that my aunt forced me to do this."

"Tamara's mom?" Ava asked.

"Yeah. She my dad's sister. She thought it would be a good idea," PJ confided. "You know, for college applications and—"

Before he could finish, the final whistle blew and Tamara stormed over. "What are you saying to her?"

"No worries, Tam," PJ said. "Just coaching a bit." He winked at Ava.

"You're supposed to be helping me, not Ava. That's why Mom pulled strings to make you our assistant coach," Tamara protested.

"I can help both of you," PJ insisted. "In fact, the two of you need to—"

"PJ!" Tamara's voice was so loud, several girls on their team turned to them with interest. "It doesn't work like that."

"I'm aware, Tam, of how it works." PJ looked from Ava to Tamara and then up into the stands at Mrs. Baker. He sighed. "You want my advice? Just play the game."

CHAPTER SIX

"Mom!" Ava caught sight of her mom as she emerged from the locker room after the game. She ran to her and hugged her. If she hadn't been in the school hallway, she would have wrapped her legs around her mother in the full-body hug she'd done when she was little. "I missed you. You were gone forever!"

Laura Sackett laughed. "Only a week, honey. But yes, it felt like a long time."

As they drove back home, Mrs. Sackett told her about the other artists she'd met at the retreat, and Ava filled her in on her tense return to the basketball team.

"That's not good timing," Mrs. Sackett mur-

mured, adjusting her sunglasses from the Texas glare.

"What's not?" Ava had explained all her fouls and Tamara's bad attitude. PJ's deception remained her and Alex's secret.

"An interview with your father came out today on TexasHighSports." Mrs. Sackett chewed her lip worriedly.

"Coach talked to them on the phone the other night," Ava said.

"Yeah, well, whatever he was trying to say didn't come across or they misinterpreted it. It's not good," she said.

Ava quickly pulled up the site on her phone. At the top of the page, a bold headline screamed:

WHERE HAVE ALL THE PLAYERS GONE?
SACKETT BRUSHES OFF INJURIES

Coach Michael Sackett of the State Championship Ashland Tigers should be riding high this spring with his young, talented team, yet we have received reports that practices are lackluster at best. Sackett finds himself with a roster that's severely depleted by injuries. Football is dangerous, even at the high school level, and will never be injury free. However, the Ashland players "are dropping like flies," according to one anonymous Ashland fan. "We've lost six out of twenty-two players, and most of those kids were starters."

At last week's practice, three players watched from the sidelines with crutches. In addition, quarterback Dion Bell is still recovering from a concussion, which has deeply concerned the parents of several players, so much so that they have pulled their sons from the program. Ashland is also seeing numbers drop at the youth level.

When reached for comment, Sackett belittled the seriousness of the situation, saying, "All teams experience this kind of thing."

Is Sackett too focused on winning and not enough on the welfare of his players? According to Doug Kelly, father of starting quarterback phenomenon PJ Kelly, who is currently out with a strained knee, Sackett's unrelenting conditioning drills are the cause of his son's injury. "Winning is good, but not at the risk of injury and permanent damage," Kelly said. "We need to make the sport safer."

Once again, Sackett failed to express concern when Kelly's injury was brought up. "The boy will heal," he remarked.

But at what cost? we ask. Wake up, Sackett! These injuries can be prevented, especially in a nongame situation. Let's hear what you have to say, Ashland!

Ava started to scroll through the comments. "Don't do that. Seriously, Ava, stop. People are mean," Mrs. Sackett said as she pulled into their driveway.

"This article is false. Coach cares about his players so much. How can anyone believe this?" Ava cried.

"I know that. But for some reason, people delight in tearing down winners." Mrs. Sackett opened the car door. "Mr. Kelly likes to stir up trouble, that's for sure."

Ava stayed in her seat and fumed. Mr. Kelly's accusations were outright lies. She and Alex had heard him and PJ. She couldn't believe she had started to like PJ just a few minutes ago! How could he and his father do this?

She suddenly sprang out of the car. She needed to talk to Alex. They had to tell Coach that Mr. Kelly was playing him.

"Where's Alex?" Ava smelled a pot roast cooking when they entered the kitchen.

"Tommy was going to pick her up from Lindsey's house on his way home from the mall. He said something about picking up an engraved birthday gift for Cassie." Mrs. Sackett pulled lettuce, a cucumber, and tomatoes from the refrigerator that had magically been filled. Her mother must have been home a while. The house was clean and tidy, too. "Do you know what he got her?"

"A silver bookmark, which makes no sense to me, but I guess she likes to read." Ava shrugged. "He had the store engrave something sappy on it."

"I think that's wonderful." Mrs. Sackett grew quiet.

Coach Sackett's tightly controlled voice floated in from the family room. "That's not what I said, Mr. Ganes. I have always followed all rules of safety."

"Your dad's obviously on the phone. Why don't you help me make a salad?" Mrs. Sackett suggested.

Ava was shredding lettuce when Coach stalked into the kitchen. He frantically typed on his phone.

"All okay?" Mrs. Sackett asked hopefully.

"Far from it." Coach waved his phone. "I'm being flooded by e-mails, and the phone keeps ringing."

"No one can really believe that you don't care about your players," Ava said. "That's just crazy."

"I don't think they believe that. At least, I hope not. They're concerned for their sons' safety, and rightly so, after Mr. Kelly accused me of pushing the boys too hard," Coach said.

The house phone and his cell rang simultaneously.

"Don't answer," Mrs. Sackett suggested. "Let this whole thing cool down."

"I can't do that, Laura. The parents deserve to hear from me." He began to walk away. "I'll be in my study."

Coach stayed in his study for hours. He didn't come out when Alex and Tommy got back. He didn't come out for dinner. He didn't come out when Tommy drove Alex to the library for a club meeting.

The phone kept ringing and ringing. Each ring shot through Ava like an electric shock. Each ring reminded her that PJ and his father were liars. And that she and Alex had become liars too.

"Don't worry," Mrs. Sackett assured her as they cleaned the dinner dishes. "Your dad will work this out."

Then Coach appeared downstairs. He wore his navy suit, a crisp white shirt, and a dark orange tie. Ava only saw him in a suit when they went to church on Easter morning. Coach hated suits as much as she hated thick tights. He looked odd without his Tigers polo shirt and cap.

"Why are you dressed like that?" Ava asked.

"I need to go out. There's a meeting at the school." Coach tightened the knot of his tie.

"What kind of meeting?" Mrs. Sackett demanded. "It's Monday night. And it's late!"

"They called a special meeting of the school's athletic board to discuss my behavior." His voice sounded strained. "They want me to explain my off-season training methods and my plans for continued player safety."

"I'm coming," Mrs. Sackett announced abruptly.

"Laura, they won't let you in the meeting," he said.

"I don't care. I'm coming anyway. Just let me throw on a dress." She hurried upstairs. "I'll only be a minute."

"Can I come too?" Ava asked.

"No," Coach said. "Tommy and Alex will be home in a few minutes. It may turn into a late night."

Ava gulped. This had become very serious very fast.

She thought about the twin promise. She was sure that if Alex were here she'd let her break it, just this once. Alex wouldn't want Coach defending himself against Mr. Kelly's lies without even knowing that they were lies. Ava *had* to say something.

"PJ didn't hurt himself practicing football. He fell off a dirt bike." The words tumbled out. "He pretended it was overconditioning, but his injury had absolutely nothing to do with you."

"How do you know this?" Coach asked. "Did he tell you this?"

"Not exactly." Ava explained how Moxy ran away and how they'd ended up hiding in the Kellys' yard. She told him they'd seen the dirt bike and heard Mr. Kelly warning PJ not to tell Coach and that they'd even gone to a Dr. Chang in a different town.

As she spoke, Coach's brows knit together and his mouth hardened into a line. She decided to leave out the part about Saint Francis. She didn't think PJ would ever leave the Tigers, and Coach looked angry enough as it was.

"You are one hundred percent sure about this?" he asked.

"Completely." Ava watched him dial his phone.

"What did I miss?" Mrs. Sackett appeared in a simple royal-blue dress. Ava wondered when her parents had acquired so many clothes in the school colors.

Coach held up a finger, then disappeared into the family room. Ava dove into her mother's arms and explained what she had confessed to Coach. Two minutes later he returned. "I just spoke to Dr. Chang. He can't give me any specifics, because he needs to respect his patient's privacy, but he did confirm that PJ came to see him last week."

Ava nodded. "Now what?"

"Now, your mom and I are going to make a quick detour to the Kellys' house for an overdue conversation. Then we are going to the school." He gave her a stern look. "You and Alex broke your promise and lied. When I return, we will have our own conversation."

Mrs. Sackett bent down and kissed Ava's head. "Fill Tommy and Alex in when they get home. And don't stay up if it gets late."

Ava knew she'd never sleep without finding out what happened.

"Do you want to stop by and say hi to Cassie?" Alex asked her brother hopefully. "We could ring her doorbell and surprise her."

"She has a big chemistry test tomorrow. She's studying now." Tommy concentrated on making a left turn out of the library parking lot. "Why would *you* want to visit Cassie?"

"No reason." Alex stared out the window at the darkened storefronts. Should she tell Tommy? Would he help?

In the library, she'd decided she would fix this weird thing with Corey, and they'd go to the movies on Friday just like they'd planned, and then her friends would never have to know anything about this mortifying day. It would be a snap . . . if only she could understand why he'd been so cold to her at lunch. She couldn't think of anything she'd said or did. She'd barely spoken to him since they'd planned to go to the movies. The whole thing made no sense.

Maybe it was a strange one-day blip. Maybe his mac-and-cheese had been poisoned. Maybe an alien had invaded his body.

Then Alex had decided that Cassie probably possessed some older-girl-with-a-boyfriend insight. And that was her big plan—to talk to Cassie. But that wasn't happening tonight.

As they waited for the one traffic light in

Ashland to turn green, Tommy let out a huge belch.

"Gross!" Alex cried. "That one smelled bad too!"

Tommy grinned and belched again, louder this time. He loved annoying Alex.

Alex held her nose as Tommy burped along to the song on the radio. Tommy was going to be no help here. She doubted Ava would either. She was running out of options. As soon as they reached their house, she hurried inside. "Mom?"

"She's not here." Ava was snuggling with Moxy on the sofa. She turned down the volume of the TV. "Neither is Coach." She told Alex and Tommy what had happened.

"Oh, wow, man." Tommy sat next to Ava.

"You shouldn't have told Daddy without me," Alex protested. "I have a phone. You could have texted."

"I had to make a quick decision," Ava said. "I was scared that Coach would get into big trouble or even lose his job."

"Really?" Alex hadn't considered this. She sat too. Together the three of them watched a cooking competition show. Alex knew that if Tommy was watching TV with them and not locked in his room playing his music or texting with Cassie, he thought the situation was serious. Alex forgot all about Corey and thought about her dad instead.

Finally Moxy barked excitedly, and the front door swung open.

"You're all still up," Mrs. Sackett said, reaching down to greet Moxy at her heels.

"What happened?" Tommy demanded.

Coach Sackett loosened his tie and threw his suit jacket over the back of the big armchair. "A lot of noise, that's what. Everyone had something to say."

"But you're okay, right?" Alex asked. "I mean you're keeping your job?"

"You father is fine. He's a great and safe coach, and folks here know that." Mrs. Sackett kicked off her shoes and perched on the arm of the sofa. "Well, everyone except the Kellys."

"Did you confront them?" Ava asked. "Mr. Kelly so deserves it."

"We had a discussion," Coach Sackett said simply. "I explained that although I am against dirt biking for my players, I wasn't so much upset about the injury. What upset me is the lack of trust. A team is like a family, and in a family there is trust, honesty, and loyalty. PJ failed to show me any of those when he lied about his injury."

"Is he benched?" Tommy asked.

"No. PJ's in a knee brace, so he can't play anyway. Benching doesn't send the message," Coach Sackett said. "But for the spring season, he will no longer be team captain."

"Seriously? You took away his captain title?" Tommy jumped up. "Did he freak?"

"PJ was upset, sure," Coach said. "Mr. Kelly was livid."

"No one's ever been kicked off as captain." Tommy shook his head in disbelief.

"He must be crazy mad," Alex said.

"I told him we'd revisit it for the fall season, if PJ shows me he can be trusted. There's no room for lies in my football family." Coach landed his gaze on Alex and Ava. "Or in this family."

Alex readied herself for her dad's lecture. When they messed up with their mother, she could be awfully loud, but she got over it quickly. Coach simmered. Alex dreaded his disappointment and lectures more than her mom's outbursts.

"We never meant to eavesdrop," Alex said.

"We felt weird tattling—that's why we didn't tell you about PJ," Ava put in.

"What I can't understand is why you left our street when I clearly told you not to," Coach said.

"Moxy ran," Alex said. "She went after a rabbit."

"She did," Ava backed her up. "Moxy runs fast, and we had to chase her."

"But did she run from our street all the way to the Kellys' house?" he asked.

"Kind of." Alex twisted her hair with her finger. She tended to do that when she wasn't telling the truth. "Are we punished?"

Coach and Mrs. Sackett carried on a silent conversation with their eyes.

"We are going to sleep on it," Mrs. Sackett announced finally. "It's late now, and I, for one, have had an exhausting day. Up to bed, all of you. We'll revisit this in the morning."

In the bathroom they shared, Ava and Alex washed up at their side-by-side sinks.

"That wasn't too bad," Ava remarked.

"We'll see." Alex wasn't letting Ava off so easily.

"I'm sorry, Al," Ava said. "Let's talk to Mom in the morning. You can tell her all about Corey. She's a softie for that stuff. I bet she'll go easy and not ground you and you can still go out."

Tell Mom all about Corey? Alex almost let out a laugh. Where should she start? That she was the only one of her friends without a boyfriend, and when she finally got the boy she'd liked forever to go to the movies with her, he blew her off for no reason? And even if she managed to fix things and get him back into movie night, now she might be grounded!

"Whatever," she said angrily to Ava, even though she knew none of that was really Ava's fault. Then she stormed to her room and shut the door.

Ava winced. *It's not like Alex to be so mean,* she thought as she turned out the light and went to bed.

CHAPTER SEVEN

Every time Alex glimpsed Corey's dark-red hair down a crowded hallway the next morning, she found it hard to breathe. She wanted to talk to Corey, yet she was scared to talk to Corey.

The anger and confusion she'd felt yesterday had transformed into a nervous, fluttery ache. She liked Corey. *Really* liked him. What if he wasn't just having a bad day? What if he really didn't like her anymore?

She buzzed on high alert all morning, barely absorbing anything the teachers said in her classes. At lunchtime, Alex hovered in the cafeteria doorway, watching her usual table fill up. Lindsey, Emily, and Rosa sat. So did Kal, Xander, and Corey.

She was sure that Corey hadn't told anyone that he'd dumped her, because none of her friends had mentioned it. Even if he'd told one of the guys, it would've trickled down to her. So she still had a chance to turn it all around. Maybe he wouldn't even remember.

"Let's go," she whispered to herself. She was determined to sparkle. She adjusted her stretchy pink headband, flipped her hair, and strutted, more confidently than she felt, over to the table.

"Look! I brought brownies." She lifted the lid of the container she held to reveal the powdered-sugar-dusted brownies she'd gotten up at dawn to make. It had been a good morning in their house. She and Ava hadn't been grounded—they were let off with only a warning—and her dad had made blueberry pancakes. Ava hadn't brought up Alex's meanness the night before. Deep down, Alex knew she had been a little harsh and that Ava was right about telling Coach. She was so worried about the Corey situation that she wasn't thinking straight. But she would make things right with Ava—just like she was going to make things right with Corey.

"Why the brownies?" Xander asked, reaching for one.

"I felt like baking," Alex said lightly. She passed the box to Corey. He hesitated, then passed it to Emily without taking one. Alex bit her lip nervously.

"You look so pretty," Rosa said. "Why are you all dressed up?"

"I'm not. I just thought I'd go for a little panache." Alex had paired her navy skirt with a kelly-green sweater that had a stiff white collar. She thought it made her eyes look super green.

"Another fancy word!" Emily giggled.

Alex cringed. Hadn't she decided not to do the vocabulary thing in front of Corey?

"What's it mean?" asked Rosa.

"'Panache' is French. It means extreme style," Alex said.

"Alex can't help it, Emily. Don't you know? She's *way* more sophisticated than any of us," Corey said suddenly. Unlike Emily's teasing tone, Corey's words had an edge to them.

Alex laughed, but even to her own ears it sounded fake. "Oh, please! I already told you. I'm not so sophisticated." She sat next to Emily and pulled out her lunch. "So I was thinking. There's a new mini golf place in Hyland. The website says it's glow-in-the-dark. Should we *all* go?"

"We could wear neon shirts," Lindsey said, getting into the spirit.

"I rule at mini golf," Kal bragged.

"What do you think?" Alex eagerly directed the question to Corey.

Corey sneered. "I think mini golf is too baby-ish for you."

Now Alex was completely confused. Who did Corey suddenly think she was?

"I bet high school guys don't go mini golfing with their girlfriends," Corey continued.

"What?" Then something clicked. "Do you mean Tommy? He and Cassie don't do anything sophisticated. They just go for ice cream and watch Netflix."

"Hey, Alex, did you know that a ton of middle school girls have a crush on your brother?" Rosa called from the other side of the table.

"Really?" Her brother was such a goof. But the other girls at the table agreed.

"It's like a disease around here," Corey muttered.

"Yeah. Why do girls like older guys?" Kal asked.

"Uh, because they're older, and they aren't so awkward and annoying—they're more mature." Lindsey rolled her eyes with the obviousness of it.

"News flash, Lindz. Johnny is only one grade ahead of us," Emily reminded her.

Lindsay shrugged. "He's still better than a seventh grader."

"What's with all you girls?" Corey's voice trembled with exasperation.

"Not *all* of us," Alex corrected.

"Oh, yeah, right." Corey shot her an angry look, then pulled out a folder of worksheets and buried his face in it.

Lindsey, Xander, and Kal continued the debate about girls liking older guys, but Alex couldn't get past the glare Corey had shot her way. She felt as if she had opened a book to a random page and was supposed to unravel the plot. Why was he angry with her?

A lump formed in her throat. She and Corey were not going to happen, and she didn't understand why. It was so unfair. She shoved her uneaten veggie wrap back in her bag and stood.

"I just remembered I have to talk to Ms.

Palmer about student council." She left before anyone could reply.

Across the cafeteria, Ava chewed the last bite of her sandwich and examined the newest photo of Chester.

"I think Chester has a crush on Carmelita," her friend Kylie McClaire confided. "Can't you see it in his eyes?"

"Who's Carmelita?" Ava studied Chester's soft brown eyes.

"She's being boarded at our ranch temporarily," Kylie said. "She has a beautiful tawny coat. I wish I could ride her." A few weeks earlier, Kylie had fallen off one of her horses and broken her leg pretty badly. She was still using a wheelchair at school, but she was so upbeat about everything that Ava sometimes forgot about her injury.

"Are you sure horses can have crushes?" Ava asked.

"Of course! Chester is totally into Carmelita. Obsessed, really," Kylie replied confidently. She'd spent her whole life on the ranch, surrounded by horses.

Ava's phone buzzed, and she quickly glanced over at Mr. Antonucci, the teacher on lunch duty. He joked with Andy Baker and Logan Medina at the far end of her table. Phones were supposed to be off during school, but Mr. Antonucci had his back turned. Ava slid her phone discreetly under the table and sneaked a peek.

The text was from Tommy. That was weird. Her brother never texted her—especially not during school.

Insanity here! Read this!

Ava clicked on the link he'd sent.

Breaking News! Kelly Departs Tigers for Saint Francis Falcons

The short article revealed few details, reporting only that PJ Kelly had formally announced today that he was switching schools—and switching football teams.

He actually did it! Ava thought incredulously. Unbelievable! Why would PJ toss away a state championship team? There was no guarantee Saint Francis could build its so-called super team.

Then she realized that the article never mentioned the super team. Was it a secret? Did only she and Alex know about it? Would they try to steal other Ashland players? She tried to puzzle this out.

"Ava." Kylie nudged her.

Ava blinked, slowly growing aware of the increased chatter around her.

"Everyone's talking about your dad!" Kylie whispered.

Other kids must have also been on their phones, because the word of PJ's defection had snaked its way throughout the cafeteria. Exclamations of outrage and shock echoed.

"Coach Sackett did this!" Andy Baker exclaimed.

"How?" asked Logan.

"Coach took away PJ's status as captain. That's the same as kicking him off the team," Andy said, his already pink skin growing red with outrage.

"Coach Sackett just lost us our best player," grumbled Owen Rooney.

"My uncle says his practices are brutal. He

was totally unfair punishing PJ," Andy ranted.

"He should get in trouble for sending our best QB to another school," Logan put in.

"Oh, he will." Mr. Antonucci jumped into the conversation. "The Tigers will lose, and it'll all be his fault."

"And get this! With Kelly gone, Tom Sackett will be QB1! That's Coach's son!" Kal Tippett hurried over from a different table to join in.

"What about Dion Bell?" Xander asked.

"He's still hurt, so Tommy gets it. I bet Coach planned this from the very beginning," Kal reported.

"Hey!" Ava stood to tell them to stop talking trash about Coach. Coach had never planned this. Tommy must be horrified to be thrust into being the first-string quarterback. He was barely comfortable playing third string!

Suddenly all the other conversations swirling about the cafeteria reached her ears. Andy and his friends weren't the only ones blaming Coach. Everyone—even the teachers—seemed to think that innocent PJ had been forced out by Coach.

She wanted to stand on the table and yell that PJ and his father were lying, that they were traitors. But would anyone believe her? Or would they just think she was defending her father? She scanned the room for Alex. She needed her twin.

But Alex wasn't there.

CHAPTER EIGHT

Ava did the mature thing. She ignored Andy Baker and his friends. She said nothing to all the kids in her afternoon classes who wrongly speculated about why PJ had left the Tigers. She knew that Alex would tell her to keep it together and not overreact. But if she heard one more snarky comment about Coach, she'd surely burst.

She hated doing the mature thing.

"Where's Alex?" she'd asked all their friends. No one knew. She finally cornered Emily before eighth period.

Emily shrugged. "Maybe still at student council? She ran off during lunch."

Had Alex been upset about PJ and Coach too?

She wasn't still so mad at Ava that she wouldn't come talk to her about it . . . was she?

"The girls' basketball team will have an early dismissal today for an away game. All players please report to the bus now." The announcement crackled over the loudspeaker. Ava realized she'd have to wait until tonight for a chance to talk to Alex.

As Ava stepped onto the team bus, Callie called out, "We need to beat them. We have to show them that even with PJ, they're still losers! Am I right?"

All the girls cheered.

"Who are we playing?" Ava asked.

"Saint Francis Prep," Madison said with a grimace.

Ava groaned. Of all the teams to be playing today!

She moved down the aisle past Tamara. Tamara stared out the window, lost in her own thoughts. Seeing her made Ava think about PJ, and that made her angry all over again. Tension on the court was already bad between them. How would they ever be able to play together now?

Ava took a seat beside Madison. She popped

in her earbuds, pretending to listen to music, and texted Coach.

how are you??? is it bad there? on bus to game now.

Don't worry about me, pumpkin. Play hard.

aren't you coming?

Coach had promised he'd watch her game today, since he'd missed the others.

Sorry. Lots to deal with here & not the best place for me to be seen right now.

Of course, Ava suddenly realized. Coach couldn't very well walk into the Saint Francis gym today. PJ had ruined Coach's team, and now he'd messed up Coach coming to watch her play!

When they reached the end of the long, winding driveway leading to the red-roofed school, a huge purple-and-white banner greeted them. FIGHTING FALCONS WELCOME PJ KELLY!

Ava hated seeing PJ's name up on the Saint Francis sign.

"Wow. They had that made fast," Madison commented. "Didn't he just decide today?"

Ava knew PJ hadn't just decided today. This move had been in the works for a while. This was crazy. She wished she'd been able to find Alex earlier. What good was keeping this a secret?

"We should pull it down. That'll show them!" Callie rallied the group.

"No! Don't do that." Coach Rader stood even though the bus hadn't stopped. "No vandalism. Got it? We're going into that school with our heads held high."

"Who'd want to go to this stupid school anyway?" Callie asked, as they filed through the halls and into the gym. "I'd hate to have to wear a uniform."

"Their dark-purple shirts aren't so bad," Tamara pointed out.

"Personally, I am *never* wearing purple again. As a protest," Madison declared. "Saint Francis stole PJ from us."

"The way I heard it, PJ left us." Jane waved her hand at the shiny gym floors and digital scoreboard. "He obviously wanted fancy. The bleachers even have individual cup holders!"

"That's cool, don't you think?" Tamara said.

"Not really," said Callie.

"Do you *really* think PJ will like it here?" Madison asked Tamara.

Tamara opened her mouth to say something, then closed it. She busied herself with the zipper of her warm-up jacket.

"Fancy does not win games, girls," Coach Rader sternly reminded them. Ava's dad said that often too. "Not on the football field or on this basketball court. Let's go! Tiger warm-ups."

They began to stretch. "One, two, three! Tiger roar, right!" called Coach Rader.

As the team cheered and moved right, Tamara stretched left. Ava watched her out of the corner of her eye. With each tiger roar, Tamara's face drained of color.

"Are you okay?" Ava whispered.

"Like you care!" Tamara's face crumpled, and

she fell out of her stretch. She choked back a sob, then dashed out of the gym.

"What's happening?" called Coach Rader.

"I'll go get her," Ava offered, chasing after Tamara.

She found Tamara in a side hall. She had slid down between the fancy water fountain and a door leading to the parking lot. Ava sat, pulling her knees to her chin just like Tamara.

"Why are *you* here?" Tamara asked.

"I came to check on you," Ava said. "You're upset about PJ, right?"

"Like you know the half of it," Tamara muttered. "I figured you'd be celebrating. You're going to get what you want."

"Huh? What do I want?" Ava turned to her.

"To be the big basketball star. When you get to Ashland High, I'll be long gone. You'll have the court to yourself. It'll be the Ava Sackett show." Tamara kicked the floor so hard, her sneaker left an angry gray scuff mark.

Ava gulped. Had she been that obvious about trying to play better than Tamara? She hadn't thought Tamara cared.

"Why are we talking about high school?" Ava asked. "That's years away."

"Not for me. I'm in eighth grade." Tamara refused to look at her.

"And you don't want to play basketball? But you're so good—"

"You're not listening!" Tamara cried. "I am playing basketball. Just not at Ashland High. No more Tiger roars for me."

"Why not?" Ava asked, confused.

"Isn't it obvious? Haven't you figured out my family by now? The Kellys and the Bakers are obsessed with sports and winning." Tamara grimaced.

"Well, yeah, I knew that. That's why your uncle decided to move PJ to Saint Francis, to help him get into college and the pros and all that."

"You know about the way it happened?" Tamara turned her gaze to Ava.

Ava nodded slowly. She hadn't meant to share their secret without talking to Alex again, but she didn't want to lie to Tamara.

"Uncle Doug thinks he can control the Saint Francis coach, and he thinks that's better for PJ," Tamara explained. "Your dad won't always listen to him, and Uncle Doug hates that. My mom hates that too. And now she's talking about having me and Andy move to Saint Francis next year."

Ava wasn't sure what to say. "Uh . . . the purple shirts are nice."

Tamara rolled her eyes. "The purple shirts are lame. I don't want to leave. I want to be an Ashland Tiger. Ever since the first time I held a basketball, I wanted to be an Ashland Tiger."

"Can you talk to your mom? I'm sure she'd understand, if you just tell her—"

"Seriously? You have no idea. Trust me. There's nothing I can do once Uncle Doug and my mom put things in motion."

"That's the truth." PJ stepped toward them. He must have come in through the side door. His assistant coach whistle hung around his neck, but he didn't have on a Tigers jersey. Or a Falcons jersey—he wore a plain olive-green T-shirt.

The emotions she'd been holding in all day swirled together and propelled Ava up and forward. Her eyes flashed darkly at PJ. "You are making a *huge* mistake, you know. My dad is the best coach you will ever have!"

"Probably," PJ agreed.

Ava blinked at his calm response, but she

kept going. "You lied to him. You lied to every-one. And not only about the dirt biking. I know about the super team *and* your secret practice."

"I never wanted to lie to him. You've got to believe me, Little Sackett." PJ leaned against the wall. "The thing's out of my hands."

"What's that mean?" Ava demanded.

"My dad is in charge. He has a plan for my future. He says this move is best for me." For a long while, PJ stared at the scuff mark from Tamara's shoe on the floor. "All I want to do is play football. Do you get that? I just want to be out there with the ball. That's the best feeling."

Ava nodded. So did Tamara. They both knew that feeling.

"We need to do something," Tamara said to PJ. "Something major."

"Beat Saint Francis today," PJ said.

"What good will that do?" asked Tamara.

"Probably nothing for me. But it will sure feel good, don't you think?" PJ smirked mischievously. "And if you wipe them off the court, Aunt Carrie may think twice about sending *you* here, Tam."

Tamara brightened. Then she regarded Ava warily. "They're a good team. You in?"

"So in," Ava said. She turned to PJ. "I'm still

mad at you. Nothing will change that."

"Yeah, I know. Your dad is furious too." PJ sighed. "It's a mess."

"What you did makes me *really* want to beat Saint Francis," Ava said.

"Go for it," PJ encouraged her. "I mean it, Little Sackett. You and Tam can be great together. Forget the other stuff out on the court. Just play your game."

"Just play your game—that's another one of Coach's sayings," Ava remarked.

PJ nodded. "I know. It's a good one."

Alex sat high in the stands, took a gulp of her peach iced tea, and then placed the bottle in the purple plastic cup holder so she could clap for Tamara's awesome free throw. The middle school basketball game had been extremely close since the start, with only two points dividing the teams in each quarter. She leaned forward to watch Ava catch a pass from Tamara, then send the ball back so Tamara could score again. The Ashland fans cheered when the team finally pulled ahead at the end of the fourth quarter.

"Go, Ashland!" cried Hallie LaVersa, Whitney's sister. Whitney's mom joined in, igniting the rest of the fans in a Tigers chant.

"We're going to win! Why aren't you cheering?" Alex asked her mom. Mrs. Sackett had been sitting silently next to Alex for the entire game, even though Ava had scored many times.

"I'm trying to stay under the radar." Mrs. Sackett discreetly eyed the other parents in the stands. There wasn't a huge crowd, but the ones who'd showed had been loudly whispering nonstop—and they all whispered the same thing. Coach Sackett had driven poor PJ Kelly to leave. He'd been wrong to take away PJ's captain title. He overreacted to dirt biking. The Tigers were sure to lose in the fall.

"Block them out." Behind them Mrs. Baker shrilly confirmed the other parents' worst thoughts about Coach Sackett, and Alex rested her hand on her mom's arm to keep her from turning. "They don't know what they're talking about."

"It's not easy," Mrs. Sackett confided, tucking her long, wavy hair behind her ears.

Alex wanted to turn and tell Mrs. Baker that PJ was a liar. She was sure Ava was dying to tell her too. A few of her friends had told her that Ava had been looking for her. Alex felt bad about not seeing Ava in school, but she'd hidden in the bathroom and in Ms. Palmer's room during class changes to avoid Corey in the hallways. And Lindsey and Emily, too. His blow-off had been so mortifying!

"Rush her, Tam! Go strong!" Andy Baker's raspy yell carried throughout the gym.

Andy sat up near his mother. Greg and Tim Fowler sat with him. Alex tried to ignore them. She watched Tamara fake left and pass the ball to Ava. The Fowler twins were good friends with Corey. Should she say something to them? What?

"You seem a million miles away from this game," Mrs. Sackett said.

"Just thinking about something. Not Daddy . . . just something else."

"A boy?" her mom asked.

"How'd you know?" Alex blushed. Her mom seemed to always clue in to what she was thinking.

"I'm familiar with the look." Mrs. Sackett grinned and perked up. "Is he cute?"

"Very." Alex hesitated to say more. Then she saw how eager her mom was to listen to something besides the gossiping parents. "It's Corey

O'Sullivan. He asked me to go to the movies."

Mrs. Sackett raised her eyebrows. "A date? I don't know how I feel about that."

"You don't have to feel anything. It's not a date. Not now. And anyway, it was a group thing. But now it's not. At least, I'm not part of it anymore." She kept her voice low, so the Fowler twins couldn't hear.

"You've lost me," Mrs. Sackett confessed.

Alex explained the Corey confusion the best she could.

Mrs. Sackett leaned in closer. "Alex, you've never been afraid to speak your mind. Don't change now. You need to stand in front of Corey and ask him why he canceled."

"Maybe I'll ask Emily to ask him. Or Ava," Alex suggested. "That's easier."

"I think he owes *you* an explanation, not your friends," Mrs. Sackett said. "That's the only way you'll understand what happened."

Alex wasn't sure she could do it. Standing in front of the boy she liked and demanding to know why he didn't like her back would be the most humiliating thing ever. And she'd already been humiliated enough for one day.

CHAPTER NINE

The Ashland fans stamped their feet and rattled the metal bleachers as the girls' basketball team closed out the game four points ahead of Saint Francis. Alex whooped watching Ava and Tamara jump simultaneously for an in-the-sky high five.

Ava's definitely a better sport than I am, Alex thought. She wasn't sure that she could be friends with any of the Kelly or Baker kids now, let alone keep passing the ball back and forth. As it was, she refused to greet Andy and his mom as they walked past.

"I don't want chicken again," Andy was saying to Mrs. Baker. "All you ever make is chicken."

"Everyone wants something different. Do I look like a restaurant?" Mrs. Baker grumbled.

"Tim and Greg are going to the food court in the mall. Can I go?" Andy asked.

"How will you get home? Yoo-hoo, Tam!" Mrs. Baker waved wildly to Tamara. "We're supposed to go to Uncle Doug's later."

"Corey's going to be there, too. I can grab a ride from his mom and meet you at Uncle Doug's," Andy said.

Alex's ears pricked at the mention of Corey's name. Corey would be at the mall. Should she ask her mom to go to the mall too?

She shook her head. Reality check! She couldn't talk to Corey at school. Did she really think it would be any easier in front of Andy Baker in the mall food court? She needed to talk to her friends first.

"We need to swing by the high school," Mrs. Sackett told Alex and Ava as they drove away from Saint Francis. "Your dad is letting Tommy and Luke borrow his car, so we'll pick him up. Warning—he's in a foul mood."

Alex met Ava's gaze from the backseat. Once again, they didn't need words. They silently agreed to tell him the rest of their story. He had to know that the Kellys had planned PJ's football move before the dirt biking accident.

"At least you beat Saint Francis," Alex whispered to Ava.

Ava nodded. She knew what Alex meant. Coach's foul mood would definitely get worse.

When they reached the high school parking lot, Tommy and Luke were in Coach's car, waiting to go. Their sneakers tapped the dashboard to the bass line of the reggae music blaring out the car's open windows. Mrs. Sackett pulled up alongside them and called Coach, but he was stuck in an endless meeting with the athletic director.

"Change of plans," Mrs. Sackett yelled to Tommy. "Your dad needs more time."

"No way!" Tommy turned down the volume. "Cassie's birthday is tomorrow. The store messed up the engraving once. I need to get there."

"Tommy, it's been a long day—"

"Please, Mom. We've got to help Tommy out. It's for his *girlfriend*." Alex emphasized this fact. Tommy was shy. The fact that he had a girlfriend was a huge deal in itself; the fact that she was as cool as Cassie was mind-boggling. Alex wanted them to stay together.

Mrs. Sackett sighed. "Okay. Leave the car here for your dad, and I'll swing you over to the mall. Grab your books out of the backseat."

"Me too, Mrs. S?" Luke called.

"You too." Mrs. Sackett liked easygoing Luke. The whole family did. And Alex used to more-than-like him, but she was over that now. He was too old for her!

Tommy hurried into the front seat. He tossed a pink coat into the back.

"Hey, careful with my coat!" Alex cried. "What are you doing with it?"

"Pink is his color," Luke teased, as he slid in beside Ava. "Tommy was thinking he'd add pink ruffles to his jersey this season."

"Yeah, because I'm not enough of a target after PJ bailed on us," Tommy grumbled.

"I must've left the coat in the car the other day," Ava put in.

Alex smoothed out the sleeves and slipped it on. "You messed it up."

"No, I didn't," Ava shot back.

"Yes, you did," Alex couldn't help herself. When Ava started, she just had to finish.

"Girls!" Mrs. Sackett cautioned, and Alex and Ava shared a smile. If they were annoying their mom with their bickering, things were back to normal.

A few minutes later, they pulled up to the main entrance of the mall. "You boys be fast. I'm going to drive down the street and grab a pizza. You dad loves the supreme pie. It may soothe the sting of the day."

"Can I come too? I'm great at shopping. I'll make sure Cassie's present is perfect." Suddenly Alex felt bold. It had to be fate that she was here. She should go talk to Corey.

"Count me out. I'm sweaty, and I hate the mall," Ava said.

Tommy hurried Luke and Alex to Magic Memories as Mrs. Sackett drove off. The small store was decorated in pink and black and featured a variety of silver items that could all be engraved.

"Oh, look at this." Alex held up a silver-backed hairbrush that had been monogrammed. "You should have monogrammed something for Cassie. I think monograms are classy. What's Cassie's middle name?"

"No idea," Tommy admitted.

"What kind of lame boyfriend are you?" Alex asked. Her middle name—Wright—was her mom's maiden name. ASw. Alex loved the way that looked. When she was older, she planned to monogram everything in her home—the plates, the towel, and even the toilet paper. She'd seen monogrammed toilet paper in a catalog once.

"Want to know the kind of lame boyfriend Tommy is? He can't even get a bookmark engraved right," Luke teased.

"That was not my fault. Can you believe they engraved 'Our story begs together'?" Tommy said.

"What does that even mean?" Alex asked.

"He's begging that she doesn't break up with him!" Luke laughed.

"It means nothing. They made a mistake," Tommy said.

"What were you aiming for?' Alex asked.

"'Our story begins together,'" Tommy said. "Get it? It's a bookmark, and we just started going out."

"I like it. Deep, yet romantic." Alex nodded. "Impressive. Total approval."

"Thank you." Tommy gave a deep bow.

"Except Lover Boy has horrible handwriting," Luke put in.

"They got it right this time," Tommy said, as

the clerk in retro black-framed glasses presented the newly engraved bookmark for inspection.

Alex proofread the bookmark. "Perfect! She'll love it."

"Would you like me to wrap it?" the clerk asked.

"Definitely," Alex answered for Tommy. She'd spied the shiny pink-and-black wrapping paper and the matching organza ribbon. Tommy could never wrap better on his own.

"It's going to take about ten minutes. Cool?" The clerk pointed to a pile of presents another clerk was wrapping.

"Very cool," Alex answered again. Now she had time to find Corey. "Listen, Tommy. A friend is at the food court. I need to tell him something."

"Text him." Tommy counted the money in his wallet.

"It's not that easy. I need to see him. I'll be superfast. I promise," Alex said.

Tommy eyed her suspiciously. "Mom will freak if I let you wander around the mall on your own."

Alex pointed at Luke. "I'm not on my own. Luke will come with me."

"I will?" Luke asked.

"Please," Alex begged.

"Sure. Taking the Sackett twins to the food court seems to be my mission in life." Luke grinned.

"Ten minutes," Tommy warned. "You better be at the entrance then or you are on your own explaining this to Mom. I am not getting blamed."

Alex hurried Luke through the mall. Her eye landed on a mannequin wearing the cutest striped sundress and hoodie combo in the window of Spruce, but she kept moving. Shopping would have to wait. She was on a mission.

She slowed as they neared the food court. She immediately spotted Corey's dark-red hair, Andy's spiky blond crew cut, and the Fowler twins' floppy brown bangs. It didn't hurt that they were all dressed in identical Tigers jerseys.

"So are we going to eat?" Luke asked. "I've got some cash."

Alex bit her lip. Could she drag Luke with her to talk to Corey or would that be weird?

Weird, she decided.

"See that guy over there?" She pointed to Corey. He stood with the guys by the curly fries stand. "I'm going to run over and talk to him. It's kind of private. Could you, uh, hang back?"

Luke wiggled his eyebrows. "What is going on here? Are you going to start engraving bookmarks too?"

"Far from it," Alex assured him. She tightened her coat around her, as if shielding herself, and headed toward Corey.

Tim spotted her first. "Hey, Alex! What's up?"

"Nothing. Just shopping." She dug her hands into the pockets. "Uh . . ." She took a deep breath. "Corey, can we talk?"

Corey studied her for a moment, then shrugged. "Sure."

She tilted her head, indicating that he should step away from his friends.

"Ohhhh! She wants privacy!" Andy made gross kissing noises.

Alex rolled her eyes. Andy was such an idiot.

She stepped behind a stand-up sign advertising tropical smoothies. Corey followed. Luckily, Andy stayed back with Tim and Greg. Now that she was here with Corey, she felt her nerve going. She studied the pattern of rhinestones on the toes of her ballet flats.

"So?" Corey prompted.

She raised her head, and they locked eyes.

Oh, wow! She thought about how great his eyes were for the millionth time. Dark blue like the water in a swimming pool on a cool day.

"So." Alex had no idea where to begin.

"You wanted something?" Corey leaned against the sign, and they both watched it teeter. He steadied it.

"I wanted . . ." What did she want? She wanted to go out with him. "Do you like me?"

"What?" Corey startled at the directness of her question. She was startled by it too. Had she really asked *that*?

"I mean, I thought you liked me." For a moment, her statement hung large in the air.

Corey's face flushed. "Yeah, well, yeah."

"Yeah?"

"Yeah." Corey studied the list of ingredients in the tropical smoothie.

He liked her! He did!

"So? I mean, what happened?"

"It's just that—"

"Alex." She felt a tap on her shoulder. She spun around to find Luke pointing to his phone. "We need to go."

"Oh, hi. One minute, okay?" She turned back to Corey.

Corey stared at her, his face filled with disbelief. Then he frowned.

"It's just . . . ," she prompted him. Finally she was going to find the answer to the mystery.

"It's just nothing. He's waiting." Corey's voice came out icy.

"But . . ." Alex fumbled, acutely aware of Luke listening to every word. "So . . . are we good?"

"No." Corey shook his head, then walked away. When he joined Andy, Tim, and Greg, they immediately left the food court.

Alex started after him, but Luke stopped her. "Tommy is waiting with your mom and Ava. We've got to go."

Alex watched Corey. He never looked back.

"I don't get him," she said quietly to Luke.

"Boys are weird," he agreed.

Ava waited until Coach swallowed his first bite of supreme pizza before she spilled the story of the super team and the Kellys' deception. As she spoke, Tommy and Mrs. Sackett exclaimed and ranted, but Coach stayed silent. He merely nodded and chewed thoughtfully.

Ava wasn't sure what this meant. She shared a questioning look with Alex. "I'm sorry we didn't tell you this part before."

"We never thought he'd leave. We didn't want to upset you over nothing," Alex added.

"Bad call. PJ's leaving sure isn't nothing," Tommy quipped. "Maybe if Coach knew, he could've stopped him."

"We're really sorry." Ava glanced at Alex. She was sure her twin would be angry with her, but she had to ask. "Are we in trouble?"

"It goes back to trust and honesty," Coach said.

"We get that. We *really* do," Ava said. She wondered why Alex was staying silent. Why wasn't she fighting harder not to be punished?

"How about you girls make dinner one night this week?" Mrs. Sackett suggested.

"Totally!" Ava smiled at Alex. That wasn't bad at all. Her twin had to be happy. Now she could go to the movies with Corey.

"PJ should try some trust and honesty," Tommy muttered.

"I talked to him today," Ava said, reaching for another slice.

"PJ? Why would you do that?" Tommy cried.

"Everyone at school froze him out."

"He was at my game," Ava explained. "You know, he didn't seem super excited about transferring to Saint Francis. His dad is making him do this. You should talk to him, Coach."

"Look, there's nothing I can do if Mr. Kelly has his mind made up, and believe me, I've tried. All day, I've tried. I'm not calling PJ blameless. The boy is almost eighteen, and he needs to start making himself heard, but I don't live under his roof, so I don't know how things are done at his home." Coach turned to Tommy. "Neither do you. There is no reason not to talk to him."

"But what about the super team?" Alex asked.

"My team won state—if that doesn't make us the super team, I don't know what does," Coach scoffed.

"I'm telling the other players about this. They can't keep thinking that you forced PJ off the team," Tommy said.

"That's so unfair," Alex protested. "I mean, logically, why would the coach force his best quarterback off his team?"

"Oh, thanks!" Tommy clutched his heart. "Nice to support your brother."

"I didn't mean that you weren't—"

Tommy jumped in before she could finish. "Dion is coming back next week. He's been cleared to play. He'll be QB1 now. All's good. I'm happier at number two."

"You know, you have the talent to play QB1 if you would only apply yourself and focus," Coach started.

"Yeah, yeah." Tommy stopped him. Ava—and Coach—knew his heart wasn't fully into football. He loved playing piano and making music, too. But now wasn't the time to get into that.

"Do you think other players will go to Saint Francis too?" Ava asked. "If Mr. Kelly said they're looking to recruit a new team?"

"I hope not." Coach folded his napkin and sneaked a piece of crust to Moxy under the table. "We'll have to wait and see."

"We can't wait! We need to do something to make sure they all stay," Ava said. Suddenly she was angry at herself for not jumping in earlier. Maybe she could've made PJ stay. He seemed like he wanted to.

"It's hard to compete with Saint Francis," Alex pointed out. "Did you see the water fountains in their halls? They have buttons to choose different flavors of water!"

"Seriously?" Tommy's eyes widened. "I heard they give every student a customized laptop *and* a watch-computer!"

"I bet they buy the students robots to do their homework, too," Mrs. Sackett added with a laugh.

"And program the robots to do the football practice sprints," Tommy suggested. "If they do that, I'm in!"

Ava listened as her family laughed and poked fun at fancy Saint Francis. She wondered what PJ and Tamara would make of them. She tried to imagine dinnertime with Mr. Kelly and Mrs. Baker and gave a little shudder. She was glad she was a Sackett.

Then she had an idea.

"You know how you said the football team is just like a family?" she asked Coach. "We should make the guys part of our family too. We should invite them to dinner. You haven't had a team-bonding event in a while."

"That's actually a good idea," Mrs. Sackett said. "I think it would do the team and the town good to see Michael Sackett relaxed and off the field."

"I can cook," Coach offered.

"Me too," Tommy chimed in.

Ava wrinkled her nose. "I think not."

"I have a better idea. We can have a big barbecue here in our backyard." Alex jumped up and found a pad of paper and a pen. "Okay, how many hamburgers will a team of football players eat?"

"You'll make your famous chocolate chip cookies," Mrs. Sackett told Coach. "We can even make the barbecue a monthly thing."

"Tommy's jazz trio can play music," Alex suggested.

"Should we invite PJ?" Ava asked after they'd planned the menu.

Coach shook his head. "That ship has sailed. Let's concentrate on the boys who are committed and focused."

But Ava wasn't ready to give up on PJ just yet. There were still six months until the first fall kickoff. Maybe she could find a way to get him back. Maybe Alex would help. Alex was good at fixing things.

Later that night Ava pushed open Alex's bedroom door. "Hey, Al!"

"Knock much?" Alex lay on her bed, reading her English book. She scooted over for Ava to join her.

"That went okay, right? No grounding." Ava rested her head on Alex's pillow. She reached for Alex's stuffed bunny and began to toss it. She couldn't help it. Whenever she saw the bunny, she just had to toss it.

"I was kind of hoping we'd get grounded," Alex confessed.

"Really? Why?" Ava cradled the bunny and faced her twin.

"Then I would have an excuse why I wasn't going on Friday. I'd just tell Emily and Lindsey that I was grounded. I could blame Mom and Dad," Alex said.

"But why?"

Alex told her about Corey blowing her off. Not once. Not twice. But three times!

"That's harsh," Ava agreed. "But Corey's a good guy." Ava had played football alongside Corey. She'd done sprints in the mud with him and push-ups in the grueling heat. Of all the boys on the team, he'd always been one of the nicest and most easygoing. "It doesn't make sense."

"It makes sense if he doesn't like me any-more." Alex thought for a moment. "I'm going to tell everyone that my parents won't let me go to the movies. Corey hasn't told anyone yet, as far as I know, so he probably won't care what I say. We're grounded, okay, Ave? Back me up."

"Sure." Ava had gone along with plenty of Alex's crazy schemes in the past—saying she was grounded when she really wasn't was not a big deal at all. "But after everything that's happened this week with PJ and Coach, I'm not sure lying is the best idea."

"Everyone's going to think I'm a loser if I tell the truth," Alex moaned.

"Maybe they'll think Corey's the loser," Ava suggested. "For not going out with you."

"Really? Corey?"

Ava nodded. Alex had a point. Corey was one of the most popular guys in school. Everyone liked him, whereas right now, it wasn't that cool to be a Sackett.

"We can fix this," Ava insisted.

"How? I've tried," Alex put her hands over her eyes. "I'll never have a boyfriend."

Ava tossed and caught the bunny a few more times. The PJ mess involved a lot of adults and a private school with big money. She had no idea how to solve that. The Corey mess was just Corey, and she and Corey were pals. "Don't worry, Al. I've got this."

"No! Don't talk to him. It's over. I'm fine," Alex insisted.

"But—"

"Seriously! It's too embarrassing if I send my twin. It's like I'm begging him to go out with me." Alex sat up. "Promise me you won't."

Ava stood. She pulled the pink coat from the back of Alex's desk chair and draped it over her shoulders. "I kind of like this, after all. Can I borrow it again?"

"Fine, whatever." Alex gritted her teeth. "You didn't promise."

"What? Oh, that." Ava wasn't going to make a promise she couldn't keep.

"Ava!" Alex cried.

Ava twirled, watching the coat billow like a superhero cape. Then she flew out of the room.

"Promise!" Alex called.

But Ava was already across the hall and in her own room. She closed her door. She would confront Corey tomorrow.

CHAPTER TEN

"Think fast!" Tamara turned the corner and bulleted a basketball at Ava.

Ava caught it easily. She dribbled it around her legs as Tamara jogged over. "Why aren't you in the locker room?" Tamara asked. "We have practice."

"I need to do something first." Ava was waiting by Corey's locker on Wednesday afternoon, hoping he'd stop by. He still hadn't shown, and the halls were nearly empty. "Did you talk to your mom after we beat Saint Francis? Is she going to change her mind?"

"She's actually thinking about it," Tamara said. "That's pretty impressive."

"What about PJ?"

"Oh, he's leaving." Tamara fixed her braid. Ava wished Tamara didn't sound so sure.

"Well, at least for you it's not like Saint Francis is building a super team for girls' basketball," Ava pointed out.

"Exactly what I told my mom!" Tamara grinned. "You know, I had you all wrong. I thought you didn't like me, because you're a Sackett."

"I thought you didn't like me, because I'm a Sackett," Ava said.

"Oh, no." Tamara shook her head. "I didn't like you because you're *almost* better than I am."

"Almost? I'm just rusty from being injured. I am better than you—much better," Ava bragged playfully.

"Then you better bring your A game today," Tamara taunted.

"Step back, because I'll bring my A-plus game!" Ava grinned.

"Aren't you supposed to save the put-downs for the other team?" Corey sauntered over.

"They'll get theirs, won't they?" Tamara slapped Ava's back.

"When we hit the court together tomorrow, the other team will need sunglasses," Ava agreed.

"For what?" Corey asked.

"We shine so bright," said Ava.

"'Cause we're stars," finished Tamara.

"Think fast." Ava sent the basketball back to Tamara.

Tamara caught it and began to dribble toward the locker room. "Later."

Ava watched her walk off. Something had changed. She still wanted to be better than Tamara, but she also wanted to play with her and win games together. PJ had done that. He might have messed up her dad's football team, but he'd helped the middle school basketball team. Ava had a feeling she and Tamara would be a force for the rest of the season.

"O'Sullivan, we need to talk." Ava turned her attention to Corey.

He shot her a funny look. "Why are you wearing Alex's coat?"

"I kind of like it. We've been sharing this coat." Ava turned up the collar. "I think I'm rocking the hot pink—even with the jersey and ripped jeans."

"It's nice, I guess." He reached to open his locker. "Sackett, can you move? I need to get my books."

"No." Ava folded her arms.

"No?"

"I'll move when you tell me what's up." Ava had originally planned to go about this in a more subtle way, but now that she was late for practice, she just wanted answers. Alex was going to strangle her. "Do you like Alex or not?"

"What does that matter?" he asked.

"It matters a lot," Ava insisted. "To Alex."

Corey snorted. "I doubt it. She sure doesn't like me."

"Where'd you get that idea?" Ava asked.

"I have eyes. I can see. It's obvious that I'm not sophisticated enough for her." Corey shook his head in disgust. "She should go out with that older guy, if that's who she's into."

"Whoa! Hold on." Ava tried to process this information. "What older guy?"

"How should I know? But she's always with him. I bet they use big words together."

"Back up," Ava commanded. "I have no idea what you are talking about."

"I saw her twice with the same guy. I even saw them hold hands," Corey insisted. "And they were laughing together. He's in high school."

"Alex does not have a high school boyfriend," Ava said confidently.

"Maybe she never told you about him."

"Corey, I know you don't have a twin sister, but let me tell you, if Alex had a boyfriend—especially a high school boyfriend—I would know about him." Ava pushed the long hair back from her face and narrowed her eyes. "Describe what you saw."

"Both times were in the mall food court. He had blond, shaggy hair and was kind of tan, I guess." Corey leaned against his locker. "Oh yeah, she was wearing that same pink coat."

"Were they eating burgers and fries one time?" Ava asked.

"Exactly."

"Corey, I suggest you make an appointment at the eye doctor. That was me," Ava said. "I'd borrowed Alex's pink coat. I think I was even wearing her pink headband."

"You? You have a high school boyfriend?" he asked.

"No!" Ava laughed. "That was Luke. He's my brother's best friend and my tutor. We were just hanging out, waiting for Tommy."

"Well, I *was* kind of far away," Corey admitted.

"But what about the other time? I know that was definitely Alex."

"You're right, Sherlock." Ava grinned. "Alex dragged Luke to the food court to come see you while Tommy was buying a present."

"Me? Why?"

"Even though she's extremely intelligent, for some reason my sister still seems to like you," Ava explained. "Go figure."

"Really? She does?" Corey couldn't hold back his smile.

Ava nodded. "You like her back, right?"

Corey nodded, but then his face clouded. "But, wow, she must hate me now. I've been horrible."

Suddenly Ava realized that Alex wasn't the only twin who was good at fixing things. She had another idea—and this one was about to make her sister very happy.

"I can fix that," Ava assured him.

"Don't you have a basketball game to get to?" Alex asked Ava the next afternoon.

"It's an evening game. It doesn't start until

six." Ava walked quickly down the sidewalk toward the main street in Ashland. "I have plenty of time."

"But I'm not even in the mood for ice cream," Alex protested, hurrying to keep up.

"Yes, you are." Ava kept up her rapid pace.

Alex stopped walking. "No, I'm not. Let's go home. I have homework."

Ava pivoted. "You're turning down double fudge with caramel peanut-butter swirl? Mom gave me money." She waved a ten-dollar bill.

Alex did love chocolate with peanut butter. "Fine. I'll get a cone to go." She caught up to Ava. "Why are we suddenly getting ice cream again?"

"I'm trying to do something nice. Because you've been so bummed about the boyfriend thing."

"Don't remind me."

"I wasn't going to. That's what the ice cream is for," Ava said.

Alex was surprised. Ice cream pick-me-ups were more of her thing, not Ava's. "Thanks."

Her phone buzzed, and she glanced down. She didn't recognize the number.

T said you wanted to talk to me?
I'm here. C.

Then a picture appeared. Cassie holding up her bookmark.

Love it! T said you helped. Thanks!

Alex showed Ava the photo. "Look how cute! I hope Tommy doesn't mess it up," Alex said. "I like Cassie."

"Me too," Ava agreed. "Why'd you want to talk to her?"

"It doesn't matter now." Alex brushed it off. She'd been silly to think Cassie could help.

They passed the hardware store, a book store, and a boutique called Bling. The display window featured brightly colored clothes festooned with rhinestones and sequins. Alex paused briefly to check them out. Even though she loved sparkles, all that shine was tacky. The shirts looked like something her grandmother might wear.

Of course, Ava hadn't paused. Alex had to jog past the old single-screen movie theater to catch up to her. In front of Rookie's, the ice cream shop, Alex peeked through the huge picture window under the green-and-white awning that allowed passersby to see inside.

"Oh!" Alex stiffened. Was that him?

She peeked again through the window, then stepped back on the sidewalk. "Ave, I've changed my mind. Let's bail on the ice cream." She continued to back away.

"Where are you going?" Ava demanded.

"Home. Or how about we go get a slice of pizza?" Alex tried to pull away, but Ava clasped her hand.

"We're having ice cream." Ava yanked her forward toward the door.

When had her twin gotten so strong? Alex wondered. "Ave, I can't. Corey's in there."

"Who cares?" Ava tightened her grip on Alex's hand and barreled through the door, nearly knocking down a mother balancing two cones in one hand and holding a crying toddler's wrist with the other. "Sorry!"

Alex found herself standing alongside Ava in the entrance of Rookie's. The chilled air smelled of sugar cones and hot fudge. Corey sat in a booth in the far back corner. He appeared to be alone. She scanned the line of people waiting to order. Was he here with Greg and Tim? Or some girl?

She didn't recognize anyone in the line. And there were no other girls their age in the shop. She took another glance at Corey. An enormous sundae topped with whipped cream, bananas, and gummy worms sat uneaten in front of him. Her eyes drifted back toward the bathroom door slowly opening. She tightened her ponytail and readied herself to see some cool, popular girl who would be sharing the sundae with Corey. That would make sense.

I'm not going to react, she told herself. *I'm not going to care. He's nothing to me.* She fixed a blank expression on her face.

Then out of the bathroom walked an elderly woman with a shellacked helmet of gray hair. His grandma? The woman passed Corey and sat with another lady. Not his grandma.

Why do I care? she thought. *I* don't *care.* She turned her attention to the list of flavors on the blackboard. Rocky Rodeo. Lone Star au Lait. Bluebell Blueberry. But the words jumbled together. She wasn't hungry—she was still curious. She stole another glance over her shoulder at Corey.

He waved.

She blinked. She must be seeing things.

He waved again. And smiled. At her.

Alex couldn't figure out how to react.

"Surprise!" Ava whispered in her ear.

Alex turned to her sister. "What is going on?"

Ava made a big deal of shrugging. "Oh, you know what? I just remembered that I need to go . . . shopping."

"Now?" Alex gazed back again at Corey. He continued to smile at her.

"Exactly," Ava said. "That store back there. What was it? Bling? The sign said they were having a sale, and I need to get there before they run out of what I want."

"You want something in *there*?" Alex narrowed her eyes at Ava. "No, you don't. You hate shopping and you hate sparkly things."

"Well . . . still . . . got to go." And before Alex could protest further, Ava ran out the door and disappeared down the sidewalk.

For a moment, Alex wondered if she should chase her. Then she looked again at Corey. Still smiling, he waved her over.

Hesitantly, she walked toward him.

"Want to share?" He pointed to two spoons besides the melting sundae.

"Yeah?" He'd been so cold all week, and now he was grinning like he'd won a football trophy.

"Yeah." He scooted over, making room for her on his side of the booth.

She slid onto the vinyl seat beside him. She had no idea what to say. She had no idea why she was here. And why had Ava run off like that? She grabbed for a spoon and swiped the top of the whipped cream. Letting the sweetness slowly melt in her mouth, she waited.

"So, I got things messed up," Corey finally confessed. "I was mad, because I thought you liked some high school dude." He explained that he'd thought she and Luke were a couple because he'd mistaken Ava in the pink coat for her.

"Me and Luke?" Alex laughed, but secretly she was flattered. He thought she could get a high school guy to be her boyfriend! "That's why you were freezing me out?"

"Yeah. Sorry." Corey dug into the chocolate ice cream. "Ava set me straight."

Alex felt relief flood through her. It had all been a big mix-up. And Ava had talked to Corey after all. And set up this ice cream thing. She *loved* her twin!

Alex joined Corey in demolishing the sundae. "You really think I look like Ava?"

"Well, you do. I mean, I was far away. And she had on that pink coat. She was eating a burger with that Luke guy and he was holding her hand—"

"Hold up. I would *never* eat a burger!" Alex cried. "I'm a vegetarian, remember?"

"Wow! True." Corey seemed embarrassed. "I told you that I flubbed, botched, and blundered it."

"So you found the thesaurus app!" Alex cried.

"I had to. I've got to know what you're talking about if we're going to hang out."

Alex didn't know which part of that sentence she liked more—that he'd looked up vocabulary words to impress her or that he wanted them to hang out.

"You should have just asked me about Luke," she said.

"I just thought—"

"Yeah, I know."

For a few minutes, they ate in silence. She grew aware of how close he was. How he smelled more of hot fudge than laundry detergent.

"Alex?" he said quietly. She turned her head. His face was inches away. She was pretty sure she'd stopped breathing.

Then his lips softly brushed hers. For a moment, she wasn't sure if this were really happening.

But it was! Corey O'Sullivan had kissed her!

He pulled back and busied himself searching for a paper napkin that had fluttered to the floor. Finally he looked up again, his face pink from his cheeks to the tips of his ears.

Alex was still smiling. That crazy, happy smile that probably made her look like a clown. But she was too excited to care. She'd just had her first kiss! So what if things were totally out of order and it had happened before she officially had a boyfriend or been out on a date!

"So we're back on for going to the movies tomorrow night with everyone, right?" she asked Corey. "I'd been kind of psyched about our first time going out."

"No." Corey looked away. "That won't work."

Alex's stomach twisted. They had kissed. She was sure he liked her. There was no way she had read this all wrong.

"Why not?" she demanded. She had learned

her lesson about confronting things early.

"The way I figure it, we're already here together. So tomorrow technically can't be our first time going out. We would have to count it as the second time, right?" He grinned mischievously at her.

Alex grinned back. A *second* date. She liked the sound of that.

CHAPTER ELEVEN

"Will you stop that already?" Ava asked. Music and laughter carried in from the backyard as the entire varsity football team and their families enjoyed the Sunday afternoon barbecue. She piled extra hamburger buns onto a tray in the kitchen.

"Stop what?" Alex asked. She rummaged in the pantry for more ketchup. She thought she'd done such a good job planning, but she'd way underestimated these boys' appetites.

"Stop all that grinning. You haven't quit smiling all weekend," Ava said.

Alex shrugged, then smiled again. "I'm happy."

"We need more iced tea, pronto," Cassie

announced, carrying in two empty pitchers. "Why are you so happy?" She'd caught the tail end of their conversation.

"Alex has Corey-itis," Ava reported. Ever since coming home from the ice cream shop on Thursday, Alex had pranced about as if sprinkled by fairy dust. She was so happy that last night, she'd sneaked into Ava's room while Ava was taking a shower and cleaned it. She'd even hung all of Ava's jerseys in numerical order! Just because. Well, because of Corey.

"What's Corey-itis? A disease?" Cassie asked, leaning against the table.

"Alex has a boyfriend," Ava explained.

"Ohhhh, is this what you wanted to talk to me about?" Cassie patted the seat next to her.

"What about the iced tea?" Alex asked.

"Those guys out there can wait. This is *way* more important." Cassie's eyes glittered with excitement. "Tell me all about him!"

Alex sat and told Cassie every last detail about Corey. Ava was happy for Alex, but like with everything she did, Alex had thrown herself full force into this boyfriend business.

"What's the hold up?" Mrs. Sackett poked her head around the open kitchen door. She looked pretty in her white pants and tangerine-colored top, yet the wisps of hair escaping from her ponytail revealed how hard she'd been working. They'd all scrambled over the last few days to put this team barbecue together. "Alex, Coach needs those buns. The burgers are ready to go."

"No can do. They're talking about boys." Ava rolled her eyes at her mom.

"I see." Mrs. Sackett grinned. "Cassie, you be kind to my son now."

"It's not about Tommy," Cassie said.

"Hey, guys—" Coach burst into the kitchen, waving his spatula.

"It's about Alex's new boyfriend," Cassie finished.

"Whoa! Alex's w-w-what?" Coach sputtered. He tilted the brim of his Tigers cap to peer at Alex.

Alex's face reddened. "It's not like that."

"What's it like?" Coach seemed more confused than anything. "You're twelve." He turned to his wife. "She's twelve, Laura."

"Almost thirteen," Ava put in helpfully.

"Michael, everything's fine." Mrs. Sackett gently led him back outside. "It's just a term. It doesn't mean anything these days."

"It doesn't?" Coach sounded unsure.

"Definitely not. Girls today don't care about boyfriends," she assured him.

"I would make that *some* girls," quipped Ava.

"You'll change your mind, Ava." Cassie shot Alex a knowing look, as if they were part of a special boyfriend club.

"Not anytime soon," Ava said. She left Alex and Cassie composing an intricate text to invite Corey to the barbecue. Ava couldn't figure why it had to be so complicated. Why not just text, *Want to come over?* Having a boyfriend seemed like a lot of work.

Ava headed into the yard with the tray of buns. As she wound her way toward Coach at the grill, she caught sight of a football soaring through the air. She reacted by instinct. In a flash, she dropped the tray on a nearby table and jumped, arms outstretched. The ball found her fingertips, and in one fluid motion, she cradled it to her body—and then *boom!* She was on the ground. Tommy had tackled her!

She squeezed the football tighter, wrapping her body around it. "Get off!"

"Fumble! Fumble!" cried Tommy. When she refused to let go, he began to tickle her.

"No fair!" Ava screeched between bursts of laughter. "I'm never letting go!"

"Yes, you are." Tommy tickled harder. After years of brother-sister wrestling matches, he knew tickling always got her.

"Tigers never give up!" Ava cried.

At that moment, a shrill whistle sliced through the music, laughter, and conversation. Everyone froze. The boys knew the sound of that whistle. Ava did too. That was Coach's whistle—the one he used on the field.

"Hey, there, folks." Coach turned down the flame on the grill and faced the crowd of expectant faces. "I was going to make a big speech later when I brought out my Texas sheet cake, welcoming y'all and telling you how happy I am to be leading such a fine group of athletes, and I guess I'll still do that, but I just saw something that made me realize why I am so proud to call myself an Ashland Tiger."

He pointed to Ava, lying on the grass. Tommy had rolled off her. "Did y'all hear Ava, when Tommy was trying to get that football from her? What did she say?"

"Tigers never give up," answered Dion Bell.

"I'm sorry, I can't hear you." Coach cupped his hand around his ear.

"Tigers never give up!" yelled Dion.

"Louder," Coach commanded.

"Tigers never give up! Tigers never give up!" the entire team chanted together. Soon the parents joined in too. Alex and Cassie hurried outside. Ava held the football high and yelled loudest of all.

"Exactly," said Coach, once the cheers faded. "We will have our ups and downs. We will win games and we will lose them too. We will battle injuries and the loss of teammates. We will face changes. But what makes our team so fierce is our drive to succeed. As your coach, I want you to know that I believe in you. I trust you. I am loyal to you. Each and every one of you. I will never give up on my players. I hope you will grant me the same honor."

A huge cheer rose up.

Coach fidgeted with the brim of his cap, then spotted the tray of buns. "Ava, help me get these burgers passed around. And Tommy, is that your keyboard over there?"

Tommy nodded uneasily.

Ava looked over at the electronic keyboard

set up under the tree at the side of the yard. She bit her lip and glanced to Alex. Coach had never truly understood how important Tommy's music was to him. She hoped Coach wouldn't say anything embarrassing in front of the team.

"Did you all know that my son Tommy here is not only an amazing quarterback but an accomplished musician? Who's up for some music?" Coach smiled.

Tommy seemed momentarily stunned.

"Go play!" Ava nudged him. Tommy stood and hurried over to his keyboard. In less than a minute, he launched into an upbeat, jazzy tune. Several parents gathered in front of him on the grass and began to move to the music. Ava watched her mom whisper something in her dad's ear and tug him out there too.

"What's going on here?" Alex asked Ava, sitting down alongside her. They watched in amazement as Coach began to sway to Tommy's music. "Coach never dances!"

"Changes, I guess. Just like he said," Ava remarked.

"Change is good," Alex said. She flopped down on her back.

"It is." Ava flopped down next to her. Together

they stared up at the clouds in the sky.

"What do you see?" They had always looked for pictures in the clouds when they were little.

"I see a big heart and three little hearts," Alex reported, still smiling away.

Ava made a gagging noise. "Of course you do."

"What do you see?" Alex asked.

Ava watched the clouds. She wanted to say she saw a tiger. Or a tiger attacking a falcon. Something that would prove that the team would be okay without PJ and whichever other boys chose to leave. But she didn't see any animals. In fact, she didn't see anything special up there. "Maybe a bike being ridden by a witch?"

"Really?" Alex squinted. "More like a kite being flown by a wizard."

Ava watched as the breeze slowly moved the clouds across the sky. Even though dozens of people milled around them, she didn't get up. Neither did Alex.

They both knew if they stayed a little longer, the clouds would change.

They wanted to see what happened when they did.

Belle Payton isn't a twin herself, but she does have twin brothers! She spent much of her childhood in the bleachers reading—er, cheering them on—at their football games. Though she left the South long ago to become a children's book editor in New York City, Belle still drinks approximately a gallon of sweet tea a week and loves treating her friends to her famous homemade mac-and-cheese. Belle is the author of many books for children and tweens, and is currently having a blast writing two sides to each It Takes Two story.

Inspired by the originality
of the Sackett twins?
Watch a DIY fashion blogger
take on middle school
in Chloe Taylor's

Read on for a sneak peek from . . .

Check out the Sew Zoey books,
available at your favorite store!

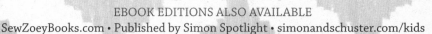

CHAPTER 1

Creeeak . . .

Thud!

Zoey Webber heard the glamorous thump of glossy paper meeting floorboards, and raced down the hall to the front door to get the mail. Only one thing could make that sound: the newest issue of

Très Chic arriving through the mail slot.

Yes!

She scooped it up along with some envelopes and interior design magazines and put everything but *Très Chic* on a table for her aunt. Then she scanned the cover to see what was *très chic* for July:

The Long (Dresses) and Short (Shorts) of Summer Style

Dots Are Hot!

25 Fresh Fashion Faces to Watch

Be Inspired . . . by BOLD Colors!

Zoey grinned at the last headline. Oh, she *was* inspired.

She was also lucky. She was spending her summer days at Aunt Lulu's house instead of the usual: being stuck at home with her big brother, Marcus, as her babysitter, or stuck at day camp for what felt like the hundredth year in a row. This summer was different. Her brother was busy with a part-time job and her dad finally agreed that she was getting a little old for day camp . . . at least if she didn't want to go.

Zoey discovered pretty quickly that "Aunt Lulu camp" was better than any day camp. Aunt Lulu ran her interior design business out of her home office, but even when she had to work, she made it fun for

Zoey. She let Zoey suggest fabrics and color combinations for clients' inspiration boards and make collages and paper doll clothes with old wallpaper samples. And if she had to go out for a meeting or something, she actually *paid* Zoey to dog-sit—which basically meant watching Aunt Lulu's fourteen-year-old mutt, Draper, snore.

Plus, Zoey and her aunt loved doing a lot of the same things: getting mani-pedis, baking cookies, reading magazines, watching old movies, and indulging in reality TV shows—they both were hands-down obsessed with fashion design competitions. Too bad Dad and Marcus couldn't stand them. "Boys will be boys," Aunt Lulu always said.

Zoey walked over to the kitchen table without taking her eyes off the magazine cover for a second. She sat down on a chair and then gently let the magazine's uncracked spine fall open to a random page. It landed on a perfume sample. It was the newest in a popular line of scents by a young fashion designer. Zoey closed her eyes and took a whiff, inhaling the amber and tuberose, and letting her mind wander. . . .

What if I were a fashion designer someday? she imagined. *I'd get to look at pretty clothes and read magazines all day long! Maybe I'd make my own perfume too, and it would smell like . . . um . . . gardenias? Yeah. And maybe one day I'd be in* Très Chic*'s "Day in the Life of a Designer" section! How cool would that be if it really happened?*

It might have just been a daydream, but it sounded pretty amazing to Zoey. She sighed, put the magazine down on the table, and began to flip through the pages, scanning each spread to make sure she saw every square inch of it.

Beep-beep.

Zoey quickly lifted her head. Did she hear a beeping sound?

Yep, that was definitely her phone saying a text had just come in!

"Coming!" she yelled toward the muffled ringtone. She stood up and looked around the kitchen.

Beep-beep.

She twirled in place. Where exactly *was* her phone? She was sure she'd left it on the table . . . but it wasn't there.

Maybe on the kitchen counter? Nope. She even checked inside the fridge.

She crawled around under the table in case it had dropped on the floor. Still no luck!

"Excuse me, Draper," she said as she gently slid her hand under his belly. Maybe he fell asleep on top of her phone? His ear twitched and his leg kicked, but his snoring never stopped. She groaned and started to get up.

Beep-beep.

Okay . . . her phone had to be somewhere . . . somewhere very close. She had spent most of the morning planted at the kitchen table drawing imaginary outfits in her newest sketchbook. It was her favorite thing to do at Camp Lulu by far.

At the beginning of summer, Aunt Lulu noticed all the fashion drawings Zoey was doing on the back of used printer paper and started hanging them on the fridge.

When there was no space left in the "art gallery," as Aunt Lulu started to call it, she surprised Zoey with a beautiful sketchbook tied with a big raffia bow. "I'm glad you're saving the Earth, but drawings like yours deserve to be on something better than scrap paper, don't you think?" she had asked. "Plus, I don't want you to lose any of them!"

And the rest, as they say, was history—soon Zoey had filled a few sketchbooks with original clothing designs. Well, some were inspired by her favorite designers, like Blake and Bauer and the amazing Daphne Shaw, especially in the beginning. But most of them were unique, and her aunt loved them all.